NEW DIRECTIONS 25

New Directions in Prose and Poetry 25

Edited by J. Laughlin

with Peter Glassgold and Frederick R. Martin

A New Directions Book

ACKNOWLEDGMENTS

Grateful acknowledgment is made to the editors and publishers of books
and magazines where some of the selections in this book first appeared:
for Edwin Brock, Scorpion Press (Copyright © 1963, Edwin Brock),
Penguin Books Ltd. (Copyright © 1966, Penguin Books Ltd.), Rapp and
Whiting Ltd. (Copyright © 1970, Edwin Brock); for Lawrence Ferlin-
ghetti, *The Sunday Paper* (Copyright © 1972 by Lawrence Ferlinghetti);
for Barent Gjelsness, *Changes* (Copyright © 1971 by *Changes Magazine*)
and *Sueños* (Mexico); for Peter Handke, *Fiction* (Copyright © 1972 by
Fiction, Inc.); for Carl Rakosi, *Academy, Identity, The North Stone
Review;* for Aleksis Rannit, *Baltic Literature* (University of Notre
Dame Press; Copyright © 1970 by Aleksis Rubulis), Adolf Hürlimann,
Zürich (Copyright © 1970 by Aleksis Rannit and Gottfried Honegger),
The Literary Review (Copyright © 1971 by Aleksis Rannit and Henry
Lyman).

"Energy Is Eternal Delight," Copyright © 1972 by Gary Snyder
"Shoot!" Copyright © 1971 by James Purdy

Manufactured in the United States of America
First published clothbound and as New Directions Paperbook 339 in 1972
Published simultaneously in Canada by McClelland & Stewart, Ltd.

New Directions Books are published for James Laughlin
by New Directions Publishing Corporation,
333 Sixth Avenue, New York 10014

In memoriam
KENNETH PATCHEN
1911–1972

CONTENTS

"ENERGY IS ETERNAL DELIGHT"

GARY SNYDER

A young woman at Sir George Williams University in Montreal asked me, "What do you fear most?" I found myself answering "that the diversity and richness of the gene pool will be destroyed—" and most people there understood what was meant.

The treasure of life is the richness of stored information in the diverse genes of all living beings. If the human race, following on some set of catastrophes, were to survive at the expense of many plant and animal species, it would be no victory. Diversity provides life with the capacity for a multitude of adaptations and responses to long-range changes on the planet. The possibility remains that at some future time another evolutionary line might carry the development of consciousness to clearer levels than our family of upright primates.

The United States, Europe, the Soviet Union, and Japan have a habit. They are addicted to heavy energy use, great gulps and injections of fossil fuel. As fossil-fuel reserves go down, they will take dangerous gambles with the future health of the biosphere (through nuclear power) to keep up their habit.

For several centuries Western civilization has had a priapic drive for material accumulation, continual extensions of political and economic power, termed "progress." In the Judaeo-Christian world view men are seen as working out their ultimate destinies (paradise? perdition?) with planet earth as the stage for the drama— trees and animals mere props, nature a vast supply depot. Fed by fossil fuel, this religio-economic view has become a cancer: uncontrollable growth. It may finally choke itself, and drag much else down with it.

The longing for growth is not wrong. The nub of the problem now is how to flip over, as in jujitsu, the magnificent growth-energy of modern civilization into a nonacquisitive search for deeper knowledge of self and nature. Self-nature. Mother nature. If people come to realize that there are many nonmaterial, nondestructive paths of growth—of the highest and most fascinating order—it would help dampen the common fear that a steady state economy would mean deadly stagnation.

I spent a few years, some time back, in and around a training place. It was a school for monks of the Rinzai branch of Zen Buddhism, in Japan. The whole aim of the community was personal and universal liberation. In this quest for spiritual freedom every man marched strictly to the same drum in matters of hours of work and meditation. In the teacher's room one was pushed across sticky barriers into vast new spaces. The training was traditional and had been handed down for centuries—but the insights are forever fresh and new. The beauty, refinement and truly civilized quality of that life has no match in modern America. It is supported by hand labor in small fields, gathering brushwood to heat the bath, well-water and barrels of homemade pickles. The unspoken motto is "Grow With Less." In the training place I lost my remaining doubts about China.

The Buddhists teach respect for all life, and for wild systems. Man's life is totally dependent on an interpenetrating network of wild systems. Eugene Odum, in his useful paper "The Strategy of Ecosystem Development," points out how the United States has the characteristics of a young ecosystem. Some American Indian cultures have "mature" characteristics: protection as against production, stability as against growth, quality as against quantity. In Pueblo societies a kind of ultimate democracy is practiced. Plants and animals are also people, and, through certain rituals and dances, are given a place and a voice in the political discussions of the humans. They are "represented." "Power to all the people" must be the slogan.

On Hopi and Navajo land, at Black Mesa, the whole issue is revolving at this moment. The cancer is eating away at the breast of Mother Earth in the form of stripmining. This to provide electricity for Los Angeles. The defense of Black Mesa is being sustained by traditional Indians, young Indian militants, and longhairs. Black Mesa speaks to us through an ancient, complex web of myth. She is sacred territory. To hear her voice is to give up the European word "America" and accept the new-old name for the continent, "Turtle Island."

The return to marginal farmland on the part of longhairs is not some nostalgic replay of the nineteenth century. Here is a generation of white people finally ready to learn from the Elders. How to live on the continent as though our children, and on down, for many ages, will still be here (not on the moon). Loving and protecting this soil, these trees, these wolves. Natives of Turtle Island.

A scaled-down, balanced technology is possible, if cut loose from the cancer of exploitation-heavy-industry-perpetual growth. Those who have already sensed these necessities and have begun, whether in the country or the city, to "grow with less," are the only counter-culture that counts. Electricity for Los Angeles is not energy. As Blake said: "Energy Is Eternal Delight."

THREE POEMS

EDWIN BROCK

THE FLAVOUR OF SPILT MILK

Threw away the ear-rings that I'd bought
her—accidentally, with potato peelings,
down the rubbish chute: a pallid marriage
cannot stand so much reality. For
half an hour we circle round each other
warily, refusing to admit the crackle of
frustration we undo. Fortunately the kids are
here: my bass growl duets with her soprano screeching
as we run barefoot about the walls and ceiling.

Adults we are—by age; normal by the standards
of normality; but in reality are not grown
so much as stretched from adolescence.

Come near us on a windy day and hear
the hum our wires make into eternity—which
we apparently inherit, as an idiot a jewel.

D-DAY MINUS

Son, you have two more months
to live. On the sixteenth of December
1963, if the hospital has guessed
right, you will begin to die. By
the time you are old enough
to read this, you will be dead:
this is a process called communication.

You will not see the world at first:
you will touch flesh and you will cry.
Years later you will cry because
you see too much and touch too little.

You will be hungry for love, and love
will feed you; later, you will be
hungry for love. And love, in case
you do not understand, is the
condition you will come to fear.

Son, you are the third of my children;
the other two are dead, looking for
love. When you meet them, be
gentle; be gentle also with me;
and she who held you happily for
nine months: we too are looking for love.

And love, in case you do not understand,
is the grandeur that will kill you.
Have children soon, my son: everyone
should live for those nine months.
Afterwards, die in good company;
for dying is a lonely occupation.

POET

You could put
four walls
around
a few words

nothing fanciful

bread
beer
sky
wave
tree
wind

a few words
like that

and work
towards them
watching

the walls
come in
as you discard

I don't know
which words
you'd discard

I don't even
know
whether you start
with the words
or the room

but I know
you'd make it

if only
you could
postpone
death
for a day
or two

WITH BILL IN THE DESERT

WALTER ABISH

PART ONE

We keep staring at the desert for hours on end. Implicit in our desire to locate the route over which we have traveled is also a longing to see what lies beyond the horizon line. In our case there's no urgency whatever in heading toward the objective, since everything, as we stand here, seems to pass us by. As may be expected, we are wearing aviator sunglasses to protect our eyes from the bright glare of the sun which dangles from a wire that is attached to the ceiling . . . But everything is quite makeshift . . . quite primitive, really, the way it should be. One need only stretch out one's hand to turn off the light . . . but we adhere to the strict rules of the desert . . . sunset at eight, and not a moment sooner. In the desert the sun sets abruptly. One moment it is light, the next you are stumbling about in semidarkness.

Are you afraid, Bill asks me.

We have known each other for a considerable length of time.

No, not really. Why do you ask?

What I said is quite true. There's little room here for the kind of fear one might experience indoors in the city. Both Bill and I contemplate starting a new city in the desert. Yes, really . . . There are a great many things that have to be taken into consideration when you build a city in the desert. For one thing, being in the desert, there's that constant preoccupation with survival. Everything one does in the desert can be attributed to a fear of running out of water, or losing one's place on the map, so to speak, and not being able to return . . . Even the most menial tasks, like cleaning the campsite, demonstrate this dependence. We take turns cleaning our campsite. Then there are the countless inconveniences of desert life . . . the sand, the occasional windstorms, the incredible heat which in no time induces a lassitude and apathy that is impossible to shrug off, the vile taste of warm water and the inadequate food . . . it probably takes years before one has adapted oneself to the exigencies of the desert. But the rewards are immense . . . Alone, the incredible emptiness that unfolds in front of our eyes each time we stand up on our feet. Actually to have infinity in one's grasp . . . to compress an awareness of each day's activity into the ever-changing undulations of the desert's surface. When the infinity beyond the horizon line is identical to what we can see in front of us, one can safely reason that infinity lies in our grasp. Elsewhere in the world it is winter and summer, and people keep falling in love with inescapable regularity. All my friends must be wondering where I am . . . I could be crossing the Empty Quarter, or the Atacama Desert, or the Dzungaria Desert, or the Arunta, or Simpson, Desert, or the Black Rock Desert, or the Painted Desert in Arizona.

There are just the two of us and the girl who comes to do our cooking. As I said before, it's very primitive. We eat out of paper plates, using our right hands to scoop up the food. Inge was amused by our lack of dexterity . . . while eating we make loud guttural sounds, and we listen closely to these sounds, repeating them over and over again. Why are we so infatuated with these sounds, I would like to know? Do they compel us to adjust our gaze upon what is most relevant for the moment? Do they remind us of the sounds camels make?

I have warned Bill that I would leave the moment I became impatient, the moment I experienced boredom . . . that was my only condition. To begin with I spent a considerable time each day thinking about my fiancée. Seeing her, again and again, as she arrived at the airport and came running toward me. She is only nineteen, and not yet aware that the desert terrain is as varied as each day's encounter with the mailman. I was attracted to her at first sight. She has long black hair and black eyes and is part Spanish, part Mexican . . . The day before I left her I explained to the best of my ability my intention of staying in the desert . . . her English is poor, and I don't know if she understood me. Everything goes on as before . . . the problems accumulate until someone solves them, or until they solve themselves. Instead of the deep blue sky, I now stare at a white stretch of ceiling. Like most things, it is filled with imperfections. I stretch out and I make myself comfortable on the floor. It is not too bad. Although I have kept my watch, I rarely check to see what time it is. We eat when we feel hungry . . . we eat when the girl comes to prepare our meals. We stare at the girl as she crouches over the alcohol stove. It is quite instinctive . . . the minute she crouches, we stare. I often wonder if my stare is like Bill's. His stare is not at all furtive. It is the stare of a man bent on acquiring information. This very moment he may be examining his hand with the same intensive curiosity. I cannot get over my fear that the blanket might catch fire. Danger is always present. One can never protect oneself from it. For example, there's the danger that with the 400-watt light bulb burning the entire day, the wires are carrying a heavier load than they were intended to, and might begin to smolder and catch fire. At night, huddled under our blankets we speak in near whispers, as caravan after caravan keeps threading its way in the darkness from one end of the desert to the other . . . In the morning, first thing after we wake up, Bill and I will thoroughly examine the terrain at our feet for evidence of their illicit crossing.

Shall we go for a walk, I ask Bill.

He mulls this over in his mind for a moment. He has to have time to think about it. His shoelaces are untied. In general, I suppose, we present a hopelessly forlorn appearance to people who set store by such things. I'm game, he says finally. How far shall we go?

Oh, a couple of miles . . . nothing too strenuous. We'll avoid the drifts. We need the exercise, we've been doing nothing but sitting here for days.

You're right. I'll leave a note for Inge just in case she comes in while we're away . . . what shall I write?

Just say we'll be back in two, three hours.

What time is it now?

It's a quarter past three.

Shall I write Inge, or dear Inge?

Does it matter?

Of course it matters, he says impatiently.

Why not dear Inge? What's the matter with 'dear'? Or do you think she'll misinterpret the 'dear'?

How can one misinterpret 'dear'? It's simply a question of form.

Exactly.

We say dear to everyone.

Some people would miss it. If you wrote: Inge, we've gone for a walk. Back in two hours, Bill. It would sound blunt. Unintentionally blunt. Far more blunt than you intended . . .

Bill looked thoughtfully into the distance, that all too familiar emptiness. Then I'll just leave out her name. I'll just write: Back in two hours, period.

As you please.

I waited while Bill searched high and low for his pencil. Then he had to find a piece of paper that was just right . . . after that, the question was raised where he should leave the note so that it would catch her eye.

Prop it up against the stove.

No, I'll pin it down with the ladle.

Fine . . .

Or better yet, I'll pin it to the pillow. He laughed softly to himself. What do you think . . .

Why not . . .

Have you got a pin . . .

I don't think so, I said cautiously. I couldn't really remember . . . Perhaps, after all, I'll prop it against the stove. He looked at me helplessly. I liked Bill, because, despite his size, despite his initiative, he was so uncertain . . . so dependent on outside advice . . .

Bill has red hair and is six feet tall. He broke his nose last August when the horse he was riding stumbled, and threw him to the ground. His nose hasn't healed properly. It is slightly askew, and gives his face a somewhat quizzical look. Perhaps the look had been there all along only I didn't notice it. It is, as I say, a matter of hunting down imperfections. One invariably leads to another. At one time Bill was in love with Leni Riefenstahl. This should come as no surprise to anyone who has seen her superbly shot and edited film of the 1936 Olympics in Germany. Bill and I watch the film almost daily. No film I have ever seen can match it in suspense or drama. The imperfections or shortcomings of the athletes are stylized, as if the losers had spent all their time training to lose.

Tonight, I tell Bill, I think I'd like to watch the high jump events, the entry of the German team who raise their hands in the fascist salute, and the scene in which the Argentinian horseman flounders helplessly in the stream after having been unseated by his horse.

Do you miss Alva? Bill asks me.

How exhilarating it is to inhale the clear bracing air as the young athletes leave their bungalows in the Olympic village early in the morning and set off for a practice run . . . Naturally, Bill and I tend to have our personal preferences . . .

Bill repeats his question: Do you miss Alva?

When I start to cry, he awkwardly, but with genuine solicitude, pats me on the back, evidently regretting that he had mentioned Alva to me. She would spread her white arms and legs and lay back as if on a sacrificial mount.

I hope you have no regrets coming to the desert, says Bill.

I can always leave, can't I, I reply petulantly.

Bill turns away, obviously disappointed with what I said.

From the very start, Bill and I had decided to discard the calendar as irrelevant to our present way of life. After all, the desert negated time. It simply made no sense to burden our stay in the desert with an awareness of time that was perfectly useless to us. Our voyage, it must be clear, was a very stationary one, and our belongings only reinforced this. There was the tarpaulin which, attached by its corners to hooks in the wall, served as our tent, and the Riefenstahl film, as well as the movie projector which was continuously overheating, and finally, there was the desert, with all its unique discomforts. We were unarmed despite Bill's protestations. I was the one who had decided against weapons. On my last stay in the desert I had stayed together with a bunch of guys in what was a former fortification. We were all extremely jumpy. At night we posted guards all around the perimeter of the fortification . . . during the daytime we quarreled about who would stand guard and when. At sunset each day I would prime the dozen or so hand grenades. I had come to enjoy inserting the three-second fuses . . . not the actual procedure, but the fuss this entailed, since everyone left the barrack for fear that I would blow myself up . . .

Bill keeps harping on my former stay in the desert. It is, in a way, the only experience we have to go by. But by no stretch of the imagination are we trying to revive, or worse yet, dress up the past. Still, I must admit that I continue to dwell on certain details of my stay . . . the discomforts were so different: they ranged from the flies that would bite us to the sudden sandstorms that suddenly, without a moment's warning, shrouded everything in a cloud of impenetrable dust.

Did you get any mail, asks Bill.

Yes . . . every few days a Piper Cub would land with the mail. Usually there was a letter for me from my fiancée . . .

Not your parents.

No . . . from my fiancée.

I didn't know you had a fiancée.

Certainly I did. Still have her letters.

Did you write her?

Oh yes, regularly. You can't expect to receive letters if you don't answer them. Though there wasn't much to write about, as you can well imagine . . .

What happened to her?

Well . . . they kept us too long in the desert. It wasn't as bad as you might think. We had a canteen which sold soft drinks, chocolates, and beer. But the beer was of an inferior quality. It was a label I have never seen again . . .

Were there any woman where you were staying?

Well . . . the canteen also served as a way station for the buses and cars heading south. There were usually one or two buses a week. Whenever a bus pulled in, we would descend from the fort just to have a look at the passengers. They would sprawl out on the folding chairs and hurriedly down a couple of beers, then the bus would take off again. Once in a while there was a woman on the bus, but generally she was accompanied by a man.

That was it?

Sometimes late at night we'd spot a light blinking in the distance. No one had the slightest idea of who it might be . . .

Your descriptions are so vivid to me, said Bill, sitting cross-legged on the floor, drawing the outlines of the city he was planning for the desert . . . I didn't think he'd keep on with it . . . The city had undergone a number of changes. Bill would spend a few hours each day working on the plan . . . it was slow work . . . The city I have in mind, he told me, should have easy access to the deep canyons . . . it will include a desert inn, a desert movie house, a large administrative building, and shops in an arcade, as well as a place where people can sell their produce . . .

A market?

Yes, a market . . . perhaps even a sports arena.

I nodded in agreement. Bill was very persuasive, and I never wished to argue with him.

Inge brought us our supper. She's only twenty-two and recently worked as a secretary. I don't know where Bill met her. Bill meets a lot of people. All he has to do is get on a bus, and he'll meet someone . . . Bill keeps complaining that Inge is too slow . . . he keeps calling her a cow, something that I resent. Of course, she does not measure up to Leni Riefenstahl. I expect Bill secretly had hoped that Inge, being a German, might evoke memories of Riefenstahl. Anyway, the less said about Inge the better. I don't know what Riefenstahl looked like . . . but it's not difficult to construct a picture of her: tall, blonde, large blue eyes, thin ankles and wrists, small breasts . . . perhaps a trifle masculine in appearance . . . certainly she would have the sense to play up her role . . . a sort of female desert fox. Inge has a snub nose, blonde hair, and blue eyes. But they are not frosty . . . I think she likes me. She does everything to comply with Bill's eccentric wishes, and even wears a desert tunic and desert shoes to please him.

How's your sex life, Inge? Bill asks her as she enters to remove the paper plates, and she, in no ways abashed, counters with: How's yours, Buffalo Bill? This broke Bill up. He kept laughing and laughing . . . I too join the general laughter . . . we have so few distractions here . . . so few things to laugh at.

What did you do today, asks Bill.

I suppose that Bill and I are accustomed to more secretive women . . . at any rate, to women who, whether it be true or not, seem to lead a second life which they keep from us. We are not terribly interested in Inge . . . Inge has become accustomed to being questioned by Bill. In fact, I think she likes to demonstrate to him her acute and critical eye, but her descriptions are too precise and factual. At ten, or thereabouts, she says, I took the Number 1 to Westwood. I was the only passenger, and the driver, a Puerto Rican, started to chat with me . . .

How do you know he was Puerto Rican, asked Bill.

Because he mentioned Puerto Rico when I complained about the cold weather. He kept saying that I should visit Arecibo . . . He came from Arecibo . . . they have fields and fields of pineapple out there . . . and then, just after another passenger got on . . . Inge laughed breathlessly . . . he asked me to go dancing with him this Saturday at the Casino . . . Dancing? Bill hooted, stamping his feet on the floor. At the Casino? Bill was enjoying himself. His laughter was contagious, and I felt myself being swept along. But where's the Casino, Bill yelled. I don't know, Inge shouted happily. For a brief moment we were united . . . the three of us by the geography of our determined laughter.

I think I'll sleep with her tonight, Bill confides to me.

What happened to your nose, Inge asked Bill . . . I tripped, he said, staring reproachfully at me. He had made no attempt to defend himself. I swung my fist at his face . . . restraining myself from repeating the same flawless arc with my hand. I do not like to contemplate change . . . it fills me with apprehension.

I watched Inge wet a handkerchief and hand it to Bill, who placed it over his nose. I was still counting on Inge to refuse . . . but who could refuse Bill? I did not refuse when he asked me to accompany him to the desert.

At eight the sun set, and the three of us were left in the darkness. They were speaking in whispers to each other. Before dropping off to sleep I thought I heard Inge solemnly say: I must warn you, I am not a plaything. I am not to be treated as an object. I felt curiously touched by her words . . . as if they had been intended for me and not for Bill.

Do you ever think about your previous stay in the desert, Inge asked me the following morning. She was lying on the blanket next to Bill, who was still asleep. She made no effort to cover her body . . . I looked at her the way I look at everything that lies in the middle distance, with somewhat startled unseeing eyes . . .

Did any caravans pass by last night?

She was trying to enter the spirit of the game. But when she lay down naked on the hot sand it was not at all like Alva . . . decidedly not. I still, sometimes, try to think of Alva . . . sweet, beautiful, mysterious Alva, who came from the country where the Aztecs plunged their stone knives into the chests of their hostages.

Today, says Bill looking at us, at me in particular, without the slightest trace of suspicion, today, we'll select a site for the city . . . He is on his feet, busy unrolling the plans, waving his hands, pointing to the horizon line . . . I think that Bill anticipated everything that followed. When Bill designed a city in the heart of the desert, it was for me, and no one else. The only thing left for us to do after the completion of the design, was to select a name . . . When Inge was out of earshot, we settled on Blitlu.

Inge keeps raging that we are ignoring her. She keeps making all kinds of unpredictable demands. Frequently we go along with her demands . . . and at night, Bill and I sleep with her. I am unaccustomed to making the necessary overtures, not out of shyness, but out of a natural reticence.

What is that over there, asks Inge in her very determined voice.

That? Bill shields his eyes with his hands as he stares into the direction she is pointing. That is too far away for me to see . . .

No, no, it's quite close . . . She keeps pointing into the distance. We feel somewhat uneasy when she points at the door. What is that?

What is what . . .

What do you call that wooden contraption that rests on hinges, and swings open when you turn the brass knob . . .

It's generally referred to as a door.

What is it doing here?

I'm going for a walk, I say to Bill. Care to join me . . . We

walked in silence for over an hour . . . a silence punctuated by her
shrill calls, her almost demented calls to us from far away . . .
until finally the sun set, abruptly as usual, leaving us to retrace
our steps in the total darkness . . .

Inge, shouts Bill . . . Inge! Inge!

I too shout her name, but our voices cannot hope to carry over
these vast stretches of desert . . .

PART TWO

The second part of Bill in the Desert is about our trip to Blitlu,
which is a picturesque oasis some four hundred kilometers from
the ocean. The sky is blue and cloudless, and the sand drifts, long
parallel ridges on either side of the straight macadam road, glint
in the bright sun as we speed by. I keep trying to read a book of
poetry Jackie had lent Bill. The poems are by Murssoyez, a black
poet, who has spent most of his adult life in Paris, and now only
writes in French. Included in the brief description on the book
jacket are a list of his other books, but the book I'm reading, called
Return to Blitlu, is the only one available in English. As the title
indicates, the poems all deal with the desert. Murssoyez writes of
his longing for the desert, and for the sight of his family and his
friends, as well as his desire to be with his fiancée who is waiting
in Blitlu. I continue to see the bleak monotonous terrain which
we are passing through the ecstatic vision of Murssoyez, who domi-
nates the desert around us with his evocation of joy as he, once
again, holds his fiancée in his arms.

Mention is also made in the poems of many places we intend
to visit. Bill and I are still wearing our aviator sunglasses, which
have come in real handy on this trip. All things considered, we
expect to arrive in Blitlu in three days. Once in a while we'll spot
a bird, and this morning as we were getting ready to leave, Bill
pointed to some animal tracks near the car. We are on our way to
Blitlu by way of Ongaru and Mesola. Mesola is 200 kilometers
out of the way, and it would seem that no one in his right mind
would choose such a circuitous route to reach Blitlu. Mesola,
today, is not even a town . . . Murssoyez mentions Mesola over
and over again . . . Thousands of years ago it was the center of

an ancient civilization, which was swept away by the desert. Now what is left of Mesola is a small group of rocky mountains that are riddled with caves in which Murssoyez claims his forefathers had once lived before they had begun to build the grandiose palaces and the elaborate monuments in the once fertile valley below. But the palaces and monuments are all gone, vanished, except for the pieces of shard and the cave drawings. In the early part of this century Mesola had still been a stop on the caravan route from Mougliot, but by the time Murssoyez was a young boy, the valley was deserted. Now, on this site, a French enterprise has built a luxury hotel with an outdoor swimming pool, and a restaurant that is described in our guidebook as being a three-star blend of East and West. That is why we are going to Mesola. Because Bill is demented . . . Because he must see it for himself . . .

Bill is half asleep at the wheel. He has no eye for the desolate terrain, or for the way the straight road splits our future in two. He sits hunched over the wheel, almost grown to it, staring at the speedometer, occasionally tapping it lightly with his index finger as he drives at a steady sixty-five, continuously attempting to break the speed record of the day before. He is pitting himself against the mileage marked on the maps we bought in New York.

Our nights are by no means comfortable, but by no means are they more uncomfortable than they had been in the past. We speak in near whispers as we lie huddled in our blankets next to the Land Rover.

How did Jackie come to invite you? I ask Bill.

She said, come and see me in Blitlu.

Just like that?

Yeah.

Did you tell her that you'd be bringing a friend along?

I wish you wouldn't keep asking the same questions over and over again, says Bill petulantly.

But what am I to do, since everything Bill tells me is totally unconvincing? I don't believe a word he says. I certainly didn't believe his explanation why Inge suddenly left us . . . and we had to cut short our stay in the tranquil desert . . . and I didn't believe him when he claimed to have run into Alva on the street, and that she had laughed hysterically when he mentioned my name.

I still think you should have been a bit more forceful with Alva, says Bill thoughtfully, looking at me.

What on earth do you mean, I ask coldly.

I think you should have explained your intention . . .

Intention? What intention? Now I was completely baffled.

Oh, go to sleep, he says.

Here I am, deep in the heart of the desert that may, at this moment, be present in the mind of a black poet . . . in the shape of a familiar map upon which a single journey can be repeated a thousand times.

Late the next day we stop in a small village that isn't even marked on our map. To our surprise it contains a small hotel that is run by an elderly French couple. The husband obligingly fetches his gun and bags a couple of birds for our supper. I try to talk Bill out of going to Mesola, but he is determined, and nothing I say will change his mind. He is taking speed, and it helps compress the great distances for him. He feels as if he has just started out. The couple who own the hotel are filled with questions. Where are you going? Who is the woman you are going to visit? How long do you intend to stay? When they see me reading Murssoyez's poems, they mention that he had passed through about a month ago. He was returning to Blitlu to visit some friends . . . At this I cannot contain my excitement. I keep thinking of his fiancée . . . see them embrace . . . Oh you know how it is with these blacks, says the wife of the owner disparagingly to me when I mention the fiancée.

All the way to Mesola, the next day, I keep thinking of Murssoyez's return. I keep speaking about it to Bill. One day, I too will return to my first fiancée, and then to my second . . . Unlike Bill, I have something to return to . . .

The sandstone cliffs of Mesola are steeper than I had expected. We drive over a dirt road into the valley. From outside, the hotel looks no different from the large and somewhat ostentatious motels that are springing up all over the United States these days. Bill parks our car next to a black Mercedes. Bill is disgruntled because Murssoyez has come between us. I change into a clean shirt while he inspects the carburetor and then the spark plugs. At least another half hour passes before he is ready.

So this is the famous restaurant, says Bill as we enter the large dining room. To our dismay we are the only guests. We are seated near a window, and during the meal we watch a short dark man in a white suit and a slim light-skinned woman dressed in a native costume, leave the hotel by a side entrance, and drive away in the black Mercedes. The waiter grins, and for our benefit makes an obscene gesture with his hand. The meal we ate came to forty-five dollars. It is the most expensive meal we've ever had. We did not want to leave any food on our plates, and when we left the restaurant we were both feeling ill. I suppose we were unaccustomed to eating so much. Bill was the first to throw up . . . Afterward we are both enormously dejected. At my suggestion we drive a couple of miles in the direction of Blitlu before bedding down for the night.

Bill flares up every time I mention Riefenstahl. I cannot resist taunting him: Well, Bill. When are you going to build your city in the desert? Every few hours Bill compulsively checks the oil, the tires, and the water. He does not complain when I read Murssoyez's poems out aloud at the top of my lungs.

The next day we reach Blitlu. On the outskirts are the usual whitewashed mud huts. I cannot contain my exuberance and excitement at being in the heart of Murssoyez's country. The black men and women are tall and good looking. The women wear brightly colored robes topped by an elaborate headdress . . . In the inner city the houses are larger, also white, with tall shuttered windows . . . and the streets are paved. Everyone we speak to tries to be helpful, one passer-by beckoning to another to have him confirm the information given us, until finally we are surrounded by eight or ten gesticulating men. She lives in the northern section, said a shopkeeper who spoke English . . . but we promptly lost our way, and were heading back to the center of the city when I spotted a large blue sign, which read: A Monument De Murssoyez . . . Deuxième A Droite.

The monument, a cylindrical polished reddish stone, stood in a small square. There was a low padlocked iron fence around the monument, but the gate was open, and inside the enclosure, when we arrived, stood a young woman. She was the first woman wearing Western clothes we had seen in the town . . . We watched as she placed some flowers at the foot of the stone. I could not read the inscription because it was in Arabic. Although the monument looked as if it had been recently erected, I still failed to connect it to Murssoyez, the poet.

Can you help us, Bill asked the young woman as she was leaving the enclosure. She spoke English with a faint trace of an accent . . . When we explained our predicament, she suggested that her husband might be able to help us. He knows everyone, she said . . . She sat next to Bill in the car, giving him the directions to her house. Blitlu, it appears, is much larger than we had expected. The northern section where she lives is by far the most attractive. Large villas surrounded by groves of palm trees . . . I mention that I had been reading Murssoyez's poetry, and wondered if the monument, where we met her, was put up for a relative of the poet . . .

No, she said. The monument is for the poet Murssoyez. My husband had invited him to stay with us. We hadn't seen him in years. He died the day after his arrival . . . It was a most terrible tragedy.

When by dinnertime her husband had not showed up, I suggested that we either continue our search for Jackie, or find a place for the night, but the women insisted that we stay . . . and after dinner had a servant show us to our room.

Much later that night I whisper to Bill: Isn't it bloody strange?

Why are you whispering, he wants to know.

Because the walls are paper thin, and every word I say can be heard in the next room.

What were you saying, he asks absent-mindedly . . .

Why did she ask us to stay?

I see nothing strange about it, says Bill. He is preoccupied with his own problems. He is worried that someone will tinker with or steal the Land Rover.

The next morning we meet our host, who is the man we saw leaving the hotel in Mesola. He asks us to call him by his first name, Henry. His wife's name is Ella. Henry smokes a large cigar, while listening with half closed eyes to the description of our meeting with his wife. I'm certain he must know that we've seen him in Mesola . . . You are looking for Jackie, Henry says to Bill. Bill

says Yes, and Henry tells him that Jackie lives close by. Only ten
minutes by car . . . but she's away in Corsica. Henry smiles at our
obvious disappointment. I know Jackie quite well. You see, she
rents her house from me . . .

Well, I say finally. We saw the great desert. We ate at the three-
star restaurant . . .

But did you see the cave drawings, inquires our host politely.
No, we were too tired . . .

When I mention how distressed I felt to hear of Murssoyez's
death, Henry abruptly inquires if Bill and I were at all familiar
with Murssoyez's work. I show him the translation I have been
reading, but Henry makes a motion with his hand, dismissing the
book. Ah, that was one of his early books . . . You must read the
later poems . . . He leaves the room, returning with two slim
volumes of poetry, handing one to me and one to Bill. Somewhat
shamefacedly, I admit that I do not speak French . . . What?
Henry with a look of exaggerated astonishment stares at me, then
turns to his wife, saying, Perhaps Ella will translate some of them
for you . . . tonight!

That night Ella comes to our room. She is wearing a long white
nightgown . . . She perches herself at the foot of my bed, which
happens to be next to the door, and proceeds to read Murssoyez's
poems. First in French, and then slowly and somewhat hesitantly,
translating them into English with some assistance from Bill and
me. We both feel acutely uncomfortable about her presence in
our room, and keep looking at the door, as if expecting Henry to
burst in at any moment. The later poems, just like the early ones,
deal with the desert. Again and again Murssoyez mentions Mesola
. . . he also mentions his fiancée, and the woman he loves. But I'm
by no means certain that they are one and the same.

Later, much later, speaking in whispers in order not to wake
Bill, I tell her about our former stay in the desert. Not my first time,
but the second time together with Bill and Inge . . . I feel so tired,
so very tired, she says almost apologetically, as she lies down be-
side me. The next morning Bill asks me if we had made love. When
I refuse to tell him, he angrily leaves the room, slamming the door
shut behind him.

After breakfast Henry drove us in his black Mercedes to the villa Jackie rented from him in the winter. It was a modern stucco building with a large terrace and a swimming pool. The pool was empty.

Had Murssoyez met Jackie, I ask Henry.

Oh yes. He was a great women chaser. I believe they met in some salon in Paris . . . I laughed, and then, his eyes narrowed as he stared at me: By the way, he asked, did my wife come to your bedroom last night to read you some of Murssoyez's poems?

I don't know if the panic I felt that moment showed on my face. Yes, I said after a brief pause. Yes she did . . . She translated a number of them into English.

Excellent, said Henry. But I cannot read the expression on his face and I don't know what he might be thinking. Had he at that moment pulled a knife on me, I think I would not have been the least bit surprised . . . instead he smiled.

Deep in my heart I know that I do not regret the death of Murssoyez . . . The only time one can ever get to know someone is when he's dead. That evening I tried to engage Ella in a conversation about Murssoyez. Henry is really the man who can answer all your questions, she said, and attempted to laugh. Henry, forever the attentive host, instantly launched into a number of amusing anecdotes about Murssoyez . . . most of them dealing with Murssoyez's love life. You must undertsand, said Henry finally, Murssoyez was a fine lyrical poet . . . nothing exceptional, but a good poet with a rather narrow range of interests . . .

Why do you keep belittling his achievements, asked Ella in a quiet voice.

My dear, I hope I haven't left anyone with that impression.

You published his books . . .

Of course . . . certainly . . . and he's a fine poet. But he was also, you will admit, something of an opportunist. He would attach himself to people in society . . . he was a good conversationalist, and would intrigue them with stories about the desert . . . But personally, he shunned the desert. He hated the discomforts, the heat, the flies, the privations . . . In Paris he was an exotic creature . . .

Excuse me, said Ella stiffly, and left the room. She gets tired so easily, explained Henry in his bland manner.

Later that evening Henry with great pride showed us his collection of Murssoyez's manuscripts and books. I counted seven books, in addition to several luxurious limited editions bound in leather. His work has been translated into nine languages, said Henry. I believe I have all the translations as well . . . you see, Ella and I were his oldest friends. I was the first man to publish his work. We were very close . . .

Before going to sleep, Bill went outside to have a look at our Land Rover. Someone, he discovered, had let the air out of the tires. I'll see to it first thing in the morning, Henry assured us.

An hour later Ella came to our room to read more poems to us. This time she slipped into Bill's bed. I hastily threw on a pair of pants and a shirt, and left the room. Henry was sitting in the dark on the terrace, smoking a cigar. Ah, he said. You've already tired of the poetry?

Yes, it's a bit heady, I replied . . . We spent an hour or so talking about Murssoyez. How did he die? I asked him.

He was killed by the brother of his fiancée. She had been waiting for him to return all these years. I believe it must have slipped his mind . . . he had so many women . . . besides, the marriage had been arranged by his parents long before he left for Paris. I feel I am partly to blame for his death since it was I who had invited him to come to Blitlu . . . He was stabbed not far from here. All of Blitlu was present at the funeral . . . I don't think I would be wrong in saying that among all the townspeople, even the ones who have never read any of his poems, there is a deep reverence for his work. I can't explain it. So with contributions from rich and poor, we put up the monument to his memory. People like you and Bill will pass it. You may never have heard of Murssoyez before, but by the time you leave Blitlu, you will never forget him . . .

Who is the woman Murssoyez refers to in his later poems?

Murssoyez was in love only with himself, replies Henry firmly.

The next day Henry took us to meet the mayor of Blitlu, a large friendly man who greeted us by saying: Ah, here are the two Land Rovers . . . Ha ha ha. Bill heatedly replies: Yes, and some bastard let the air out of our tires.

Apparently someone would like you to remain here, says the mayor continuing to laugh. The mayor's house is not as splendid as Henry's . . . It is situated near the old city, and all the rooms are much smaller.

Did you know Murssoyez, I ask the mayor.

Of course I knew him, he replies. Everyone in Blitlu knew him. That's why we put up the monument.

At dinner we ate lamb and rice, washing it down with trintola, a locally made alcoholic beverage. Henry and the mayor would frequently translate snatches of conversation, since none of the mayor's friends spoke English. Before we left, the mayor introduced us to his young daughter. I recognized her at once as being the young woman who had left the hotel in Mesola together with Henry. She spoke some English, but was extremely shy . . . When I mentioned Murssoyez, Murssoyez having become the chief topic of my conversation, I saw the tears well up in her eyes.

She was to have been married to Murssoyez, explained her father after she had hurriedly left the room. He was on his way to the wedding when someone knifed him . . . When we find the man, we will kill him. Henry, who was standing at my side, seemed quite unconcerned by the seeming contradiction between his and the mayor's version of Murssoyez's death.

I think we better be on our way.

Yes, yes, immediately, says Henry.

No, I mean Blitlu.

Tomorrow morning I'll have the tires fixed, he promises.

But the next day the spark plugs are missing. That evening the mayor brings his daughter to dinner at Henry's house. She seems far less restrained . . . I speak to her about the desert, and about my previous stay in the desert. When I stare into her large black eyes I can see the murdered Murssoyez staring back at me.

I hope we shall all become close friends, Ella says to me that evening. But that night she does not come to our room, nor does she on any of the following nights. The days pass quickly. One day the mayor comes over in his jeep and takes us on a tour of his property, which is quite extensive. I thought you would like to see what I own, he says enigmatically. It is hard not to develop a liking for him.

In the desert sunsets are abrupt. One minute it is light, the next you are groping around in the dark. Other transitions, namely departures, can be just as abrupt. We all stand at the entrance to the house seeing Bill off. The Land Rover is filled with odds and ends that Henry and Ella have given him. Just before leaving, Bill hands me the sketches of the city he is planning to build in the desert. I have nothing to give him. I am wearing a native costume, and look as if I have lived here all my life. Even the English I speak has come to sound more and more foreign to me.

That afternoon, when Ella inquires if I had asked the mayor's daughter to marry me, I know that I have finally reached the center of the desert where people understand the needs of my heart.

AUTHOR'S NOTE: WITH BILL IN THE DESERT *was written shortly after I saw a one-man show of Terry Fox at the Reese Palley Gallery in New York. Fox had placed a large square canvas, of the sort used in construction work, on the polished wood floor at one end of the 20' x 80' interior, and hung another five feet above the floor, creating a tentlike structure. In the well-lit, bare, white, windowless room the glare from the single bright light bulb dangling from the ceiling above the stretched canvas defined the area of shade beneath it. The light formed a topography of the interior that was, at once, a familiar romantic configuration in which the tent became the emotive key to a kind of disturbance of things past, and another in which one's physical presence, one's emotions, were measured (and partly activated) by one's proximity to that light. When I first saw the tent, a group of people were relaxing under its canvas roof, chatting, drinking beer, while the empty cans at their feet seemed to lie on sand. I wrote* WITH BILL IN THE DESERT *thinking of the space of the room and that of a desert. Bill and the narrator traversed both, so that I could chart the interior and exterior space, enlarging one to the size of the other.*

COPLAS ON THE DEATH OF MERTON

ERNESTO CARDENAL

Translated by Mireya Jaimes-Freyne and Kenneth Rexroth

Our lives are rivers
that flow to death
that is life
Your death is a diversion Merton
              (or absurd as a koan?)
your death trademark General Electric
and the cadaver back to the U.S.A. in an Army airplane
      with that sense of humor that is so much your own
you Merton with your corpse dying of laughter
The Dionysian initiates used to use ivy
        (I didn't know it)
Today joyfully I play this word death
To die is not the same thing as an auto collision
                        or as a short circuit
      we have been dying all our lives long
Contained in our life
      like a worm in an apple? no
not like the worm but like
ripeness!
Or like the mangoes in the summer at Solentiname
yellowing
waiting for
the orioles . . .
           the hors d'oeuvres

were never the same in the restaurants
as they were advertised in the magazines
nor the poem as good as we wanted it to be
nor the kisses.
We have always wanted more than we wanted
We are Somozas always wanting more and more haciendas
    *More More More**
not only more but also something different
    The wedding of desire
the coitus of perfect volition is the act
of death.
       We walk amongst things with the air
of having lost an attaché case
of great importance.
            We go up elevators and we come down.
We go into supermarkets, into stores
like everybody else, looking for
a transcendental product.
        We live waiting for
an infinite rendezvous. Or
           a telephone call from
the Ineffable.
And we are alone
immortal grains of wheat that do not die, we are alone.
we dream in steamer chairs contemplating
          the sea the color of a daiquiri
waiting for somebody to pass by
smile at us and
say *Hello**

It is not a dream but lucidity.
    We wander in the midst of traffic like sleepwalkers
    and go through the signals
with eyes open but asleep
we savor a manhattan in our sleep.
It is not sleep
Lucidity is the image of death
    of illumination, the blinding
radiance of death.

   * Asterisked italics denote English or French phrases in the original.

And it is not the kingdom of Oblivion. Memory
          is the secretary of oblivion
                    She works in the archives of the past
But when there is no more future but only a fixed present
all that we live revives, no longer as memories
and the whole of reality reveals itself
in a flash.

Poetry too was a departure
like death. It had
the melancholy of trains and planes that go away
                    Little station of Brenes
in Cordobita la Llana
                    trains that pass in the night
a *canto jondo* in the depths of Granada
In all beauty there is sadness
and homesickness like in a foreign country
                    *MAKE IT NEW**
          (a new heaven and a new earth)
but after that lucidity
you come back to the clichés, the
slogans.
Only in the moments in which we are not being practical
concentrated in the Useless, gone
then the world opens to us.
Death is the act of total Distraction
also: Contemplation.

Love, love above all, is an anticipation
of death
     There was a taste of death in the kisses
               being
                    is being
                         in another being
     we exist only in love
But in this life we only love for a few minutes
feebly
          We only love or exist when we stop being
when we die
                    naked of all being in order to make love

*make love not war**
that flows to love
which is life

The city which came down from heaven was not Atlantic City
    And the Beyond is not the *American Way of Life**
        Jubilation in Florida
or like a *weekend** without end.
Death is like an open door
on the universe
                    there is no sign *No Exit**
and for ourselves
                        (to travel
    toward ourselves
        not to Tokyo, Bangkok
                    is the appeal
        stewardess in kimono, *la cuisine
Continentale**
it is the appeal of the ads of Japan Air Lines)
        A Wedding Night, said Novalis
It is not a Boris Karloff horror movie
And it is natural, like the fall of apples
according to the law that attracts stars and lovers
—There are no accidents
            only a fall from the great Tree
you are one more apple
Tom
                            We leave our bodies as we leave
                    a motel room
But you are not H.G. Wells' *Invisible Man*
            Nor a ghost in an abandoned chalet
            We don't need Mediums.
And children know very well that NO exists
that we are immortals
For can napalm kill life?
        From the gas chambers to nothingness?
    Or are the Gospels *science fiction*?*
Jesus entered the room and threw out the hired mourners
        That's why the swans sing, said Socrates just
before dying.

Come, Caddo, we all go up
to the great village
to the great village
—Toward the place where all the buses and airplanes go
Not to an end
but to the Infinite
we fly toward life with the speed of light
Like the fetus breaks the amniotic sac . . .
or like the cosmonauts . . .
—the exit
from the chrysalis
And it is a *happening.**
the climax
of life

dies natalis

this prenatal life . . .
Abandons the matrix of matter
Not an absurdity:
but a mystery
a door open to the universe
and not to the void
(like the door to an elevator that wasn't there)
And already definitives.
. . . the same as waking up in the morning
to the voice of a nurse in the hospital
And we no longer have anything but only are
but we only are and only are being
The voice of the lover that speaks
lover take off your *bra**
The open door
that nobody will be able to close again
—"God who commanded us to live"
even though we long to return to
atomic associations, to
unconsciousness
And the bombs are bigger every time.
Necrophilia: flirtation with death. Passion for all dead things
(cadavers, machines, money, dregs)
and if they dream about a woman it is under the image
of an automobile.

The irresistible fascination with the inorganic
            Hitler was seen in War One
            ecstatic before a corpse
            with no wish to move
(soldiers or machines, coins, crap)
Gas chambers by day and Wagner by night
"5 millions" said Eichmann (it was more like 6)
Or rather we would make up the face of death
The Beloved Ones (don't say the dead)
made up, manicured, smiling
in the Garden of Repose of Whispering Meadows
            of *THE AMERICAN WAY OF DEATH**
        1 martini or 2 to forget that face
relax & watch TV
            the pleasure of driving a Porsche
                (any line you choose)
perhaps to await the resurrection frozen
in liquid nitrogen at −197°
                (put in storage like the seed that never dies)
until the day comes when immortality will come cheap
after coffee. Benedictine
a sport suit for the kids, to push away death
while they invent for us the serum of youth
            the antidote
for dying.
Like the good *cowboy** in the films, who never dies.
            Looking for the Fountain of Youth in Miami.
After the advertised pleasures in the Virgin Islands.
Or in the yacht of Onassis in the Lethean Sea . . .

You did not want to belong to the men with a Name
and with the face that everybody recognizes in the photos
in the tabloids
your desert which flowered like a lily was not that of
the Paradise Valley Hotel
            with cocktails in the swimming pool
under the palm trees
nor were your solitudes those of *Lost Island**
        with the coconut palms bending over the sea
*LOVE?** It's in the movies

the eruptions of eternity
were brief
—Those of us who have not believed in the Advertisements of
this world
dinner for 2, *"je t'adore"**
*How to say love in Italian?**
You told me: the
Gospels don't mention contemplation.
Without LSD
without the horror of God (or
better translate it by terror?)
His love is a radiation that kills without touching us
in a void more vast than the Macrocosmos!
In your meditation you could only see that vision
of the commercial plane between Miami and Chicago
and the SAC plane with the Bomb inside
/the days when you were writing to me:
*My life is one of deepening contradiction and frequent darkness**
Your *Trip?** it is not very interesting
this journey to vast solitudes and etxensions of nothingness
all as though made of plaster
white and black, with no color
gazing at the luminous ball, blue and pink like agate
with Christmas on Broadway and copulations and songs
shimmering on the waves of the dusty Sea of Tranquillity
or the Sea of Crisis dead to the horizon. And
like a sparkling little ball on a Christmas tree . . .

Time? *IS money**
it's *Time,** it's a limp prick, it's nothing
it's *Time* with a celebrity on the cover

And that ad for Borden's milk under the rain
many years ago at Columbia University, blazing up
and going dark, lighting up for so fleeting an instant
and the kisses in the movie theatre
the films, the movie stars
so fleeting
GONE WITH THE WIND
even though still beautiful and luminous on the screen
the dead stars are still laughing

the car breaks down, the refrigerator
has to be repaired
>   She was in a dress yellow as butter
>   orange as marmalade
>   and red as strawberries
/like an ad in the *New Yorker* and the memory
and the erased lipstick of kisses
farewells from the windows of airplanes that flew
>   to oblivion
girls' shampoos more distant than the moon
or Venus
Those eyes worth more than the Stock Exchange

Nixon's Inauguration Day has already gone by
the last TV image has dissolved
and they have swept up Washington
Time? Alfonso el Tiempo? *Is money,** mierda, *shit**
time in the *New York Times* and *Time*
>   —And everything tasted like Coca-cola . . .

Proteins and nucleic acids
>   "the beautiful numbers of their forms"
proteins and nucleic acids
>   the touching bodies feel like gas
beauty, like a bitter gas
tear gas
>   For the movie of this world passes by . . .

>   like Coca-colas
>   or sex *for*
>   *that matter**
Our cells are as ephemeral as flowers
>   but not life
>   protoplasms, chromosomes but
not life
>   We shall live again the Comanches used to sing
>   our lives are rivers
>   that flow toward life
now we only see as if we were watching TV
afterward we shall see face to face

every perception is a rehearsal for death
                                    beloved it is the time for pruning
   All the kisses that you were not able to give shall be given
           the pomegranates are blossoming
all love is a rehearsal for death
           So we fear beauty
When the Duke of Ch'in eloped with Li Chi
she cried 'til her clothes were soaked
but once in the palace she was sorry
she had cried.
           San Juan de la †   is doubling the point
           some ducks
           pass by
                       "the foreign islands"
or *desire* San Juan de la Cruz used to say
infinite desire—
                   tears the cloth of the sweet encounter
And the Thracians used to weep for births says Herodotus
and sing for deaths
—It was in Advent when at Gethsemane the apple trees
next to the greenhouse, are like skeletons
with an efflorescence of white yes like those
of the deepfreezers.
I don't believe Alfonso Cortés said to me in the Madhouse
when I told him that Pallais was dead
I think it's politics or
something like that.
Do they still bury a camel
with them for the journey? And in Fiji
the teeth of whales for their weapons?
The laughter of men when they hear a joke is the proof of their
belief in the resurrection
           or when a little child cries in a strange night
and mama calms him
Evolution is toward more life
           and is irreversible
and incompatible with the hypothesis
of nothingness
Yvy Mara ey
we went in migrations looking for it in the interior of Brazil

("the land where one never dies")
        As mangoes in the summer of Solentiname
are ripening
while the Novitiate is there under a hood of snow.
        The golden orioles pass
        to the Island La Venada where they sleep
you told me
It is easy for us to approach Him

We are aliens here in the cosmos like tourists
        we don't have homes here only hotels
Like gringo tourists
            *everywhere**
in such a great hurry with their cameras
        that they are hardly aware of what they are seeing
            and like leaving a motel room
    *YANKI GO HOME**
Another afternoon dies over Solentiname
Tom
        these sacred waters are resplendent
and little by little they go out
it's time to turn on the Coleman lantern
        all joy is union
        and sorrow is being without the others
                Western Union
the cablegram from the Abbot of Gethsemani was yellow
    *WE REGRET TO INFORM YOU etc** . . . .
I only said
O.K.
                Where the dead are united and
                    are with the cosmos
                            one
    because it is "far better" (*Philippians*, 1, 23)
["For I am in a strait betwixt two, having a desire to depart, and to
be with Christ; which is far better:
    "Nevertheless to abide in the flesh is more needful for you."]
"And as the moon does and is reborn anew . . ."
        death is union and
            already one is oneself
            and is one with the world
death is far better

the malinches are blossoming tonight, broadcasting their life
        (his renunciation is a red flower)
death is union
        ½ moon over Solentiname
        with 3 men
one does not die alone
        (his Grand Lodge of Reunion) of the Ojibways
and the world is much more profound
Where the Algonquian spirits in their spirit mocassins
hunt spirit beavers over the spirit snows
        we thought the moon was far away
to die is not to leave the world
but to plunge into it
you are the secretiveness of the universe
        the *underground**
away from the *Establishment** of this world, of space-time
without Johnson or Nixon
        there are no tigers there
                                the Malays say
(an Island of the West)
                which flows toward the sea
                which is life
        Where all the dead gather, O Netzahualcóyotl
or "Heart of the World"
        Hemingway, Raissa Maritain, Barth, Alfonso Cortés
the world is much more profound
        Hades, where Christ descended
                womb, belly (*Matthew*, 12, 40)
["For as Jonas was three days and three nights in the whale's
belly; so shall the Son of man be three days and three nights
in the heart of the earth."]
                SIGN OF JONAS
        the profundities of visible beauty
where the great cosmic whale swims
full of prophets.
        All the kisses you could not give will be given
One is transformed.
. . . "as one was buried in one's mother's womb . . ."
                as the Cuna chief said to Keeler
Life does not end it is transformed
        another interuterine state, say the Koguis

that's why they bury them in hammocks
in a fetal position
                    —an ancient doctrine, said Plato
that there are in Hades
                        people who have gone from here . . .
Beziers, and the cathedral seen from the train
            Nothing one felt nostalgia for is lost
                    the odor of the Midi
the red tower of St. James by the Tarn
the lights white and green of Paris, and those of the Eiffel Tower:
            "C-I-T-R-O-E-N"
Lax has traveled with the circus
            and knows what it means
        to raise the tent by lantern light
leaving the family home deserted
and the journey by night toward another city
and when the wife of Chuang Tzu died
Chuang Tzu didn't mourn
                Hui Tzu found him singing and dancing with
the rice pot for a tambourine
            the hammock is the placenta, the cord
of the hammock the umbilical cord
                "your headaches won't hurt"
            seed-plant-seed
the dialectic of destruction
            I say
is that of the wheat. To live
is to die and give ourselves for the sowing of life
until, masked, in white gloves, enters
the policeman
                of what Signs we don't know
And to hand ourselves over to death with love
And
if the stars don't die
they remain alone
if they do not return to the cosmic dust the stars
            seed, plant, seed
death is union
            not in Junction City
Or as the Cunas say too
            "we'd like to eat a good meal some day"

And we clamor for the deliverance of the beloved
And as Abbot Hesiquio used to say: it is
(the constant thought of death) "as
in the serene sea the fishes play
and the dolphins leap for joy"
      And, like the moon dies . . .
           They are in an island, in Haiti
            they told Columbus, they are all in an island
            eating mameyes by night
—Or the island Boluto, west of Tonga
happy and full of flowers and spiritual breadfruit
"it seems he was electrocuted"
                  Laughlin writes me
"but at least it was quick"
                    torn the film
that divides the soul and God . . .   And:
        . . . because love craves that the act should be very brief . . .
          they are going to enter
      the rivers of love of the soul into the sea
she arrived beautiful as Joan Baez in her black automobile
You used to laugh at the ads in the *New Yorker*
    here is one for Pan Am
    **Ticket to Japan
              To Bangkok
                  To Singapore
        All the way to the mysteries**
A ticket to contemplation?
    A ticket to contemplation.
                  And death.
    All the way to the mysteries
The commercial advertisements are his
manuals of meditation, says Corita
                Sister Corita
and they are advertisements of something else. Not
to be taken literally.
Biological death is a political question
of something of that sort
              General Electric, fate
                    a jet from Vietnam for the cadaver
but after the winter is gone, by Easter
or by Whitsunday
you will hear the Trappists' tractors near the cemetery

Trappist but noisy, turning over the earth
to sow new corn maidens, the ancient maize.
           —it is the time of the resurrection
                    of the Caterpillars and of locusts

Like the banana tree that dies to give fruit as the Hawaiians say.
           You were all empty
                    and having given all the love you have
no more to give
                    and were ready to go to Bangkok.
To enter the beginning of the new
to accept the death of the old
                    Our lives
                    which flow to life
the window of the great jet plane
                              was crying with joy as it took off
      for California!
At last you came to Solentiname (which wasn't practical)
after the Dalai Lama, and the Himalayas with their buses
painted like dragons
           to the "foreign islands"; you are here
with your silent Tzus and Fus
Kung Tzu, Lao Tzu, Meng Tzu, Tu Fu and Nicanor Parra
and everywhere; it is so simple to communicate with you
as it is with God (or as difficult)
           like all the cosmos in a drop of dew
this morning on the way to the latrine
Elijah was snatched away by the chariot of cosmic energy
           and in that Papuan tribe when they saw the telegraph
           they made a tiny model of it
           so they could talk with the dead
The Celts used to lend money says Valerius Maximus
to be paid beyond the grave.

           All the kisses given or not given.
That is why the swans sing said Socrates
on your breast the electric fan
is still turning
           We only love or exist in dying.
      The great final act of giving one's whole being.
O.K.

THE TRANSPARENT BIRD

OSMAN LINS

Translated by Clotilde Wilson

Without definite features as yet, an eight-year-old face. Fine, light hair covering the forehead. Leaning out of the kitchen window, thoughtfully he watches the black-and-white-spotted cat sitting on the wall. There is a hint of sadness hidden in his eyes and on his lips a trace of precocious resignation. Clearly reflected in his face, a suppressed and angry arrogance. An arrogance without firmness, a thing at once elastic and insecure—a loose spring.

"You're looking down at me because you're on the wall. But I'm going to be a man, I'm going to live a hundred years. Grow. And when I'm taller than doors and roofs, where will you be? Eh? Sitting where? As I look at you, already I see your bones shining on the refuse heap. You walk soundlessly; you're a walking silence. When I grow up my heel will strike the ground like thunder. I'll shout with a voice like a gong. And you, you proud thing?"

The cat and its profile long gone to dust, futile to seek the boy's in that man's exhausted face framed in the train window. His dark hair is turning white, his black woolen suit (in mourning for his father) is too loose, too comfortable, his white socks wrinkle at the ankles and his shoes are unpolished. In the rack over his head are his dull black brief case with papers and money, his metal-tipped umbrella and gray hat with a round-trip ticket in its band.

How many years ago in this very train did I tear up those letters one by one? And for how many years have I been seeing at dawn and dusk this same countryside? Unlike me, it has changed little. And what about the change in me? Has it been for better or for worse? How was that boy going to react during supper? How about my relatives and their vain plea for clemency? This sugar cane plantation we are passing, like all the others along the way, has the look of eternity with its sorry stack, its old roofs and dark shed. One has the impression that it is still the same men and the same little boys who are watching the train go by and that the cows in the pastures are still the same. Only the trees, because of summer and the rainy season, change in order each year to recover their youth. Happily, man's youth is not like the leaves of those trees. If it were, were I to become young again, I would surely make the same mistakes, perhaps others greater.

The dining room light is yellow and dim. Even if they put in stronger globes it would be almost the same; the city's generating plant is old and poor; short-winded, it works slowly like the city. Supper was over an hour ago, the children's three places are empty, they are asleep. Sitting at the head of the long table from which the maid has not yet removed the cups with their remains of coffee, the empty butter dish, the plates and the knives, forks, and spoons (she will do so only after everyone has risen from table, that is the rule), the man, tieless, his shirt sleeves rolled up, is listening impassively to the argument of an old woman in black. A large old-fashioned silver brooch with her deceased husband's portrait fastens the opening of her dress. Her two daughters are watching her hopefully; but it's obvious that the boy would give a great deal not to suffer this humiliation. The man feels from the other side of the table his wife's eyes fixed upon him—eyes which are never easily pleased and which seems to be crying out: "Don't listen to her, do as you've done before. Pity is costly."

Eudóxia, you're wasting your time. You're wasting your time looking at me like that, as if I were a roulette wheel about to stop at a number on which you've not placed a bet. Don't you know me yet? Haven't you become accustomed to the look of distress with which I hear complaints like this? Shall I have to imprint upon my face my inner resolve, a resolve taken long before she even thought of coming, bringing, the better to move me to compassion, her three children, and that brooch on which we see the profile of my mother's brother? I shall show no leniency, though for today, of course, I shall offer some hope. I shall have no mercy, all the papers are legal and in my favor, in a few days the house in which they are living will be mine, we shall have more means, we have children, three, we must leave them something. This woman, the boy, and the two girls will for some months live without paying in the house which they will have owned and which will not belong to them. No more than three months. In this way I shall be doing them a favor which will accrue to our benefit for several months while people still remember the facts and might therefore blame us. Those four, then, will consider me cantankerous, but not very, and even a little naïve. Then I'll evict them.

Though you may think otherwise, behold a child. Bare from the waist up, ensconced in his room in the same bed that he left two years and ten months ago—swearing to himself not to return before his dreams were fulfilled, before he could flaunt his triumphs in the face of the many mean relatives who had never believed in him— yes, the same bed that now will have to be changed because his bones have grown. He is kneeling, his back bowed, his face in the sheet, between cold hands. A rectilinear steel rod, bent by its curving posture and seemingly in intense search of its original form, a sob rises and swells within his body!

They won. It is hard to accept, and yet it is true. I lost. Once again the hateful routine, again this static city, these streets that only an earthquake would change, again the life I detest, the dull empty life to which I am condemned. I should get up, change my clothes, catch the first streetcar and go to that place with gritted teeth. Just as I did that other day. Take the leap once again, but this time with firmer resolve. I'll not go though. Why did I not resist hunger, why did I not let myself die? They would breathe a sigh of relief, content to say to themselves that I should not have destroyed myself, that I should have lived, but at heart they would have to accept the truth: "He was a man. He failed in business, in misguided undertakings, he died destitute, but he accepted the obligations of his decision. In this he won." They would not have the right to smile, to look at me with irony, compassion, condescension and a sort of satiety, as though, famished, they had all devoured my capitulation. Well, I shall accept the destiny they have given me. But they will see who came back. They will say one day that it would be better had I lived out my life far from them; for they will submit to me. I shall be the king, the master of them all.

Two faces, one derisive and solemn, in profile against the high bolster, its jaw held in a handkerchief, the other in front of it, mordant, staring at the dead man, both motionless. The profile is clean cut (it was not that way in life) giving an impression of youth despite the mustache the color of tarnished silver; the watcher, to the contrary, is aging and thus the two appear to be all but superimposed studies of the same face—the one in repose, the other strained.

So it is he, my father. Many years ago, when abandoned, I experienced his pitilessness and resolved to begin life over again, I wanted to see him just as he is now, bereft of all power and authority. Even then this corpse that was now before me dwelt within him, directing his life, establishing the laws that were to govern me. I was the grown son who must receive as heritage not only the things that man prized and acquired but also his insistence upon values which according to him represent all that is great and eternal: the warehouse, the houses to be rented, the reputation of an honest man, life without love or adventure, the city, the habit of molding the lives of others. Well, I received the heritage. I renounced for all time any personal expression of the act of living. I married the woman whom he considered meant for me, I am impregnated with everything I detest, I corrupted myself, I like to be respected, the possessor of wealth which will increase, I bear my father within me, I shall never leave this city. I am the continuator, he who submits, the son. The father.

The young woman, her left elbow resting on her right hand, her left hand kept free to gesture—her old attitude—smiles and motions toward the sea.

"At last. After so many years of waiting, I am going to cross it."

"I have seen your name in the papers. I read that you had won a scholarship to Spain. I was glad; I said to myself: Now, who could imagine she was going to become a famous artist? The paper reproduced some of your pictures, fruit, birds flying. One was transparent. One could see the bird and its heart. It looked like a bird of prey."

"That's the way people look."

"Exactly. It was terrifying. Does it exist, that bird?"

"No."

A creaking of boards, the gentle swaying of the boat, words in a foreign tongue shouted by the sailors into the wind.

"You didn't use to draw in those days."

"I used to write poems. I never showed them to you."

"Sometimes when I have a little time I come down to the harbor and stand looking at the boats. But I never go aboard. And so you are going to take a trip! I'd like to see your other pictures."

"When I have a showing, I'll send you an invitation."

"My father died some time ago. Did you know? I took over the business. I'm living in his house. The address—"

"I know. You'll get the invitation."

"I want to ask you a favor. Send me a post card from Spain. A picture of the gypsies in Granada."

"How shall I sign it?"

"Who do you think I am? Sign it as you wish. Your own name or any other. Or don't sign it."

"I'll put a man's name."

"Coming from Granada I'll know who's sending it. Well, well, who would have imagined? You know, opening a drawer one day, I too came across some poems of mine. Incredible. I didn't remember them. How people change, eh?"

"I think I haven't changed very much. If I have, it was for the better. I'm the same girl whose letters you tore up one day in the train. A little older. Even so, I think I'm prettier than I was then. Or am I mistaken?"

"No. You're not mistaken."

She had a gold tooth still, to be sure, and her skin was less clear, but her eyes were no less bright. Her hair was prettier, her breasts smaller, her waist more slender. Attractive, with something intense and ripe about her in her blue dress against the ocher wall and black roof of the warehouse. Eudóxia is younger than she. But she looks older, in her loose dresses, with her absent-minded, furtive manner, concealing her constant attitude of suspicion. With each passing year, her walk becomes slower, her eyes sharper, her mouth more greedy. This other woman, on the contrary, has changed almost not at all. Paper and pencil, paints. Imagination. She was always like that, a source of dreams. Now, because of having dreamed, she is going to Granada. Although she used to say to me: "One day we shall take a trip." *We.* I contemplate the ships at the dock; that is all I have left of the adventures we longed for when her life and mine followed the same course. And yet, we would not be happy, that unrealized trip to Spain would embitter our life together. Spain would occupy her mind like another destiny, better, perhaps, but forbidden and therefore all the more coveted. The worst of it is that she would never speak of it, but there it would be, the secret dream, forever a barrier between us. That would not do. Since she is a woman of imagination and since she makes use of it, let her devote her life to putting miserable draw-ings on paper—fruits, birds, clowns. Will she send me the color post card of the gypsy dancers of Granada? If she does, she won't put my name on it; in spite of all, she is sensible. I can rest assured.

She smiles, her gold tooth gleaming in the light from the lamp-post coming down through the branches of the fig tree; they appear to be caught, he and she, in that net of shattered fragments of darkness and radiance. Her upraised hand takes in the deserted street, the wet pavements, the smell of damp earth around them, the barking of dogs, the closed windows and doors, the lowering sky. He, with folded arms, without tie, his collar turned up, his body ill at ease in his still-new suit, short-armed, long-legged; she, with her hair in bangs, her dress nipped in at the waist and billowing out from below the hips over numerous underskirts, smelling of powder, cologne, and fresh linen. Ashamed of the tone of his voice whose inflections he himself does not always recognize and which, despite his efforts to modulate it, rarely obeys him (even less when, in excitement, as a moment ago, his words tumble over one an-other), he decides to keep still and listen to his girl.

"You may be sure I too find this a dull town. When I read the Recife papers and see all that goes on there, I'm discontented. There you can see ocean liners, princes, movie stars, they have an airport, a zoo, a public library, lots of movie theaters, military parades, streetcars, a river crossing the city, tall buildings. Paved streets. And the lampposts are very different from these. Here the rails are iron, painted black. There they're round, silver colored, with the arms of the Republic. There are public gardens with lots of benches. Just imagine what the larger cities must be like, Paris, Singapore, Manchester. If I were a man, I'd go into the navy. We'll have to spend our whole lives here in this place; it's like being in prison! But who knows but what we'll take our trip some day and cross the ocean?"

We. She said *we*. I, not you, will take that trip. Don't you know what a poet said, disillusioning the woman who was in love with him, who must have been like you and who thought she would never be separated from him. "I am Goethe!" I too am someone, I shall be a big name, I feel an inner power. Comfort, my father's money, family, native city, I'll give up everything. What I am destined to win, I don't yet know. But I do know that one day I'll come back here a famous man. Your husband will be a business man or perhaps a notary's clerk, you will have a home and children, but your greatest pride, confessed to no one, will come from having been witness to my youth. I am Goethe.

Everyone around the table under the lamps, listening to the priest's eloquence, the words so many times proffered on identical occasions about fidelity, devotion, the wedding of Cana. In the middle of the embroidered tablecloth, embellished with English china and sparkling silverware, atop the enormous cake, vaguely reminiscent of a Babylonian temple, two little dolls representing the bride and groom holding a heart on which is scrawled in silver dust the word *love*. The faces of the women, garnished with hats of diverse origins, worn out for the most part but revived with ribbon or flowers of velvet, assume a look of rapture, those of the young girls, some of whom are wearing long stockings and high-heeled shoes for the first time, are aquiver with anticipation; the men's make an effort to appear knowing and circumspect, and in the eyes and lips it is possible to find traces of irony and boredom. Above the vague cloud of hats and faces looms the father's, still with evidence, though already somewhat diminished, of his exaltation over the fulfillment of the alliance he had schemed and arranged with such skillful pertinacity and with obvious signs of annoyance at the priest's flowery talk, which seemingly would never end.

All those people in their new clothes, pretending to listen so intently, are resisting the impulse to invade the buffet and eat and drink an amount equal to the values of the presents given—useless presents, all of them, and in bad taste, that will just clutter the house and that I shall have to dispose of shortly despite Eudóxia, who can't conceive of giving away anything, no matter how worth-less. Only the priest is listening to his own words, adequate in length and commensurate with the importance of the two families and the remuneration he is being given. Those words of his, I know where they are seeping. They are not going out through the doors or windows but they are disappearing forever at my side, sucked up by this well to which I have bound myself and whose bony elbow I feel at this very moment. Without enthusiasm for anything, without friends, indifferent to everything that does not add to her fortune, she takes in everything and gives out nothing. Never does she give anything to anyone. With the passing of the years I shall become accustomed to her surreptitious ways, her tireless ambition, I shall become her slave, moved by compassion which I should feel for myself rather than for her. Why, then, those pious words, why speak of bonds that are eternal and holy? We are uniting two fortunes—and two poverties. Nothing more. It is money, inherited wealth that constitute holiness for us. And don't waste your time looking for symbols. The only valid one for us are those silly dolls displaying a meaningful word, but only a word, on a paper heart. I may not even be able to get rid of the presents we have received today.

He waited for the servants to leave before opening the drawer and rummaging among the faded folders in search of the papers. Would he have remembered them had it not been for the article in that evening's newspaper with photographs of the pictures— regional fruits, an extraordinary bird—and the name once so familiar? In the deserted warehouse, with the anxiety of one seeking an important document, he finally found them, and the eyes that had borne witness to the visions they expressed contemplated them and knew them not.

Poems. Why have I kept them so many years? They are mine and not so bad. Some nobility and depth of feeling come through. And yet, even then, I was not all purity; my heart harbored some meanness to be fostered later by my father's diligence, until today like a swarm of loathsome creatures it flourishes darkly within me. I remember how when I showed *her* the verses I had written she lingered over them. At first I thought she couldn't understand them, then I realized she was reading them with great care because she liked them. She believed in me. And yet, in the end, it was not I who broke through the shell and discovered a way to creativity and freedom. She it was who mastered the hands of her youth and made them her own. As for mine, cautious, ever closed, engendered by I know not what subtle and laborious process, in what cabinet of time, in what dark night of uncertainty have I lost them?

NINE POEMS

BARENT GJELSNESS

RITE

When the waters overflow their banks,
When The Snake
Moves through His lands
With water-moss
Pouring from his scales,
Moves through His lands
As the shuttle through the loom,
Weaving the world in green,
Then all things shall be as they were:
Leaf, fruit and vine
Swollen with light.
Four oceans grow
Like young blue suns.
The earth in joy is shaken.

THE CHANGING

Hunched forward—
Trouble in the belly,
In the head—
So many things
Permanently gone—
Hopes and objects
Vanished like smoke in wind—
Beings loved no less, and
Vanished too—
Peter caught by opium
Somewhere in India,
Wasted to his skeleton,
Writing one line about
The beauty of the meadows there.

The brush-painting—1200 A.D.—
Purple leaves and black branches—
In an instant disappeared.

Hunched forward,
Trouble all through the self,
Humming anyway,
Listening to the wind in crazed branches,
Imagining the passage into death.

STONE

In this stone I gave you,
This fire-agate flare,
Is the still center
Of the last coldness
In the universe,
Before the Wheel of Time
Begins again,
And the perfect ice
Like Antares
Breaks into flames

NETSUKE I

Netsuke,
In the shape of a foetus,
Old ivory, well polished,
No flaw
In surface or depth,
And where the head should be
A tiny horse emerges,
Forefeet legs and head,
Eternally poised in midair
Above the lower half
Of the foetus that bore it.
Who gives birth to that,
Gives birth to all
Who make
What has not
Existed before.

SO

In the late autumn
I return with a great
Circle of black-red bark
From the high mountain.
The bark is from
An immense tree
Struck down by lightning.
The bark is twice the girth
Of a giant turtle's back,
As sturdy as the skin
Of a big drum,
And as frail as an old
Tibetan parchment
In the span of ages.

LOVE POEMS: FRANCE, 1960

Like the sea . . .
In Europe, once, I felt the loss come in
And fill a little vessel called A Year
And break it. There was nothing to begin.
Like debris
Desire and memory
Were swept away, in darkness, and in fear.

The hubless wheel has turned: ten times since then.
The currents where love's fragments were
Endure beyond all lives, beyond all men.

There is a time
            To say
                    Goodbye to her.

The time is here.
The land is here. The sky.
The sea is here, which never says *goodbye*.

FLIGHT II

Leaving the bones behind,
The Bird called The Night-Wind Spirit
Soars outward over the bay.
His two heads
And two huge tails
Work as one,
As they do in all things.
Fearless,
Happy,
Flowers in his claws
And shreds of bone,

Giant bees
Winging around them,
He encompasses
Many incarnations.
He will outlast
Civilization, reason,
Imagination,
The best we've done.

PRAISE OF A TIME

We live in a long low house
On the side of a mountain.
Ivy on the house,
Green the whole year,
And a tin roof that leaks in rain.
In our bed
We listen to the spatter-dropping
All across the roof.
When the wind shifts
The tempo changes.
All around the house
Yellow stalks of slim bamboo
Rustle in rain and wind,
In sun and wind,
In the breezes
Of the dusk.
This life that comes and goes
So beautifully.
Soon it will be summer,
The monsoon season,
And the green shoots
Will grow to be
A bamboo screen
Higher than our house,
Heavy with its life,
And as lightly moving
As the rain in wind.

TRANSPOSITION

"When you gather to plan, the universe is not there."
—GERARD DE NERVAL

The weather was
Sixty below zero
When a man and a bear
Began their ancient story.

"A big-game hunting guide."
The man with his rifle
And years of practice.
The bear with his wits and fear.
And the silence,
The snow around them,
The indifferent stars.

The man,
Ever narrowing the distance,
Had been sure.
But the bear too
Was sure,
And the tracks he left
Became intricate,
Disappeared.

And then the bear
Was tracking the man.

It didn't take long.
Those who came later
Read in the snow
The end of it.

In the last seconds
The man was stalked so well
He never sensed the truth,
"His leather mitts
Still on his hands,
And the safety-catch on his rifle
Still engaged."

TWO POEMS

SONYA DORMAN

THE WOMEN OF TOWN STREET

1
opal blue windows each one
                moons out at us
yellow plastic trellis holds up
                her sweet potato vine
dying in the sulphur kitchen dust
                no one's ever home
it seems only at midnight a naked head
                hung in the center
of the plaster sky lights up
                forty watts' worth
of territory and gold moons
                on cold beer cans

2
every day's an undernourishment
out   out   the cage is too small
I won't canary for you one day more

54

the children wear down my sill
with their hungers as they enter
out   out   into the alleys over the hills
even at a slow crawl over the weeks' shale
blisters on my knees can't hurt
more than the children's little hammers
nails   nails   hold me to the wall
all of you swing from my weight

3
brown house lime green door
two shutters on the left
                    cracked locust shells
lodge in their hinges
dusty steps
                    Annie's brownboard school floor
in pink green and yellow chalk
she writes: I love Daddy
but the steps keep turning brown
how does she know which way
they go since they go
                    up and down?

4
old oak's been there on the corner
since an acorn among horse plops
    it's still there in a cracked circle
    behind the supermarket
summertimes the cold spit
from the market's air conditioner
    cools it and maybe at night
    it feels for the lettuces inside

5
crocks   jugs   stale biscuits
I route the gravel with a broom
                    on the sills

vine leaves lie among shards
of dry paint   at dawn
sunrise shines through a green gallon
    Calabrese onions hang
tattered purple
    the cat snores
nothing darkens my horizon
rain is welcome   chives blossom
while a Blaze rose bleeds
above the door
    the reason for a rose
may be obscure but at times I know
the flower is a pause between root
and hip   the reason for roots
may be the fruit but I like to think
    the flower is enough

6
the cold holds
water is dazzling in its still forms
wearing my shroud I rush from room to room
each window
a bell ringing in the sky

the winter sun
shines everywhere at once
always low and at night the Wolf Moon
blunts its fang
on the ice
someone snarls with hunger

wearing my bridle
I crawl along corridors
carry a green moon in each finger
to see myself by

also at dawn
I lie in ditches like a piece of water
in my still form
I'm dazzling

THE EIGHTH SEA JOURNAL

I wake to gold paper, white
window frames, to wonder which
clarity failed during the dream,
to worry how the clouds fared
and if the sun has come again.
With one eye on the doorway
for safety's sake, just like
waking in childhood (ghost
with runny nose), often
in despair at rain, I find
there's yet a roof over my head
and a real floor; not one worm in sight.

       ❂   ❂

Triumph of separate seasons: strawberries
for breakfast, a pair of blue herons
whose shadows swim over the lawn,
winter rinds discarded with our boots.
One by one the seeds depart, leaving me
to breathe. Last year I threw away
our girdles, lacings, gates, porcelain;
this year I grieve for those gone.
My daughter's snotty ghost
hangs in her closet like old beads.

At ten there's a message from the world.
Dear lady, may we install aluminum
storm windows against the east wind?
No. You shan't take away frames
I've lived with, no matter how I've hoped
to break them, loose the shapes,
pour out lucid as moonlight on salt water
and sing hallelujah for freedoms
I've invented.
No thanks. Keep your comforts
and I'll forge my own, boiling blood
and the child's marrow in my saucepans
into which the husband sword will plunge.

       ❂   ❂

It's too bad to squat in my garden
pulling up values by the root,
just because someone said: *you ought.*
With great care each afternoon I go back
and replant. That way, some green
continues to unfurl in my plot.
You ought to get out and see
what grows in other gardens, they say.

Hoeing my own row I feel it necessary
to take a whack or two elsewhere;
what's the good of weedlessness on my own
when around me Bouncing Bet, Solomon's Seal,
Viper's Bugloss and Oxalis thrive?
Let them spread wildly while I bum
around on the porch with my bare feet up
and vapor condenses on the bottle in hand.
There's witchweed curling over my skull.

           *   *

Northeast wind comes across the estuary.
It tunes up the television roof antenna
which sings in S-shaped waves,
sound of an enormously amplified
60-cycle hum, like pain, like shame.
As if every device in our man-made world
stood up, hairs on a scared nape,
and trembled. The throb of a cut wrist.
The live wire carrying last night's
bad speech into the future where
we'll have to face it again.

Wind snores at the listener
trapped under the thin roof of her skin.
The easy answer is to rip away
the aerial and live without pictures,
but no thanks, Gentlemen: I'll stay tuned.

           *   *

One of the evening's illusions
consists of peppercorns: dust
which I distribute to my family,
also along coastal areas where hunger breeds.
Here are the embalming peppers and corns.
Birds fly trailing sore wings
through the pines. Under those trees
peppercorns pile up like shot,
a dust which stings.
Embedded in flesh a few peppercorns
add savor to the dead.
The evening's illusion is a fat one,
like the cat with a meow in its mouth.
Now my kettles cry out.

✼   ✼

At bedtime there's the ghost
of ghost stories.
The bed floats in its frame,
a long picture. Just thinking of sleep
is too good to be true,
like catching a bird with salt.
There's that moment of bedding down,
old donkeys turning and turning
in the ammoniated straw,
asleep on their feet;
there's anticipation of lights out,
chimney voice with its whispers
of old smoke.
Here we spend half our time
recounting the spilt beads, soured milk,
wounds, spleens, and platters of dust
the world has served us.

At bedtime, clutching the mattress purse
I burrow into my home in the treasure house.
Not a worm in sight in this dark,
I say, as if writing down a dream
or catching a ghost by the ear
or putting the lost beads back
on their string without getting
my thumb caught while the wind hums
and the green curls into brown sleep.

THE DISMEMBERING OF THE DONKEY

ANNE DE SAINT PHALLE

It was night. Canby walked rapidly along the street, trunk and legs inclining at counterpoint as if his rump was a loose hinge. Lois walked beside him, furrowing her brow.

"The difference between scientific and mythical thought is that in mythical thought you're dealing with signs," Canby said.

"You mean symbols?"

"No, signs. There's a difference."

"Give an example."

"Okay. Like 'outsider.' That's a word with a limited number of referents. Some people are outsiders, and some aren't. Or 'girl.' You either are a girl or you aren't. It's limited."

"Okay, so what's scientific thought?"

"Scientific thought deals with concepts without limited referents."

"Like . . . ?"

"Well, like the wave theory of light."

They were silent for a while, still walking fast. Lois looked at a fire hydrant and thought, Some things are fire hydrants and some things aren't.

"People usually think mythically," Canby resumed. "It's like Chagall beginning to paint rabbits when before he's been painting only donkeys and horses. He doesn't change his ability to paint donkeys and horses but simply introduces a new element into his repertoire."

"Rabbits?"

Lois felt for her purse and remembered she had forgotten it.

"Right, you're right. The donkeys and horses don't change, they just have something added to them: rabbits. But when Chagall changes genres, that's a conceptual change like developing a whole new scientific theory."

"What's the analogy for writing?"

"Well, that's sort of different. It's like Joyce writing stories about old men, women, husbands, wives, every type of person except eight-year-old boys. When he does write a story about eight-year-old boys the other elements of the story don't change. The old men stay the same. But when he switches from stories to poems, the entire world of his thoughts is transformed. Nothing new is added, but everything is recast."

Canby steered Lois around a corner. A movie marquee came into view.

"Oh, I see."

"Yeah."

"It's like the change from Newton's theory of the world to Einstein's."

"Exactly," Canby said as they moved into the line. "Concepts, as opposed to signs, are like webs—if any one part is changed, everything else has to be changed. Signs can be added to forever without being changed."

"What's the moral conclusion?"

"There is no moral conclusion."

The line carried them inside, and then they could talk again.

"It's like thinking in spirals instead of in lines and planes," said Lois.

"But people resist thinking in concepts," said Canby. "They don't realize there are infinite numbers of systems beside their own. They spend their lives on one conceptual plane. When a new concept is forced on them, when Darwin tells them about evolution, when college students take over buildings, they resist the new ideas because they would have to change all their old ideas. Concepts are like hinges, junctures between different planes of thought."

"We're just rocket ships traveling from planet to planet. There is no absolute planet," Lois said as Canby pulled out his wallet.

"Yeah, and that's why there are no moral conclusions. The mind is too large for morality," Canby said as he handed Lois her ticket.

Later that night, Canby and Lois were lying on Canby's floor after several bowls of hashish. Canby stood up and switched off the light. Lois frowned.

"You're depriving us of one whole sense," she said.

"Oh, no, there's much more to see in the dark," Canby said.

He returned to his supine position and placed his hand on Lois's breast. Both hearts beat quickly while Lois lay still and Canby's fingers traveled.

"You shouldn't desire anything," Lois said finally, firmly.

Canby removed his hand. There was an unpleasant pause.

"Let's eat," Canby said. He got up, flicked on the light, and opened the bag he had bought at Elsie's. It contained two Holstein Mettwurst sandwiches and two Sprites. Lois picked up a calendar from Canby's desk and asked Canby to translate the stories under the fairy-tale pictures while they ate. The stories were in German.

When they finished Canby lay on his bed.

"Youthful asceticism . . ." he began.

"Listen, I don't go in for asceticism," Lois said from across the room. She came and sat beside Canby on the bed. "Anything that's fun is spiritual. Sex is fun . . ."

". . . but it's not spiritual."

". . . but it's what surrounds sex that is bad. You shouldn't impose your desires on someone else."

Canby turned his face to the wall. Lois lay down beside him and let her head rest against his shoulder.

"You're okay with that combat jacket on," Canby said. He kissed her and looked at her tenderly. His fingers began exploring again.

"Just think how much your body's been moving all day," Lois said. "Wouldn't you like to let it rest for a while?"

"Well, go over there," said Canby. "Leave me in peace with my desires."

"This is good practice," Lois said. She crossed the room and sat at Canby's desk. "You should be glad for every chance you get to conquer your desires."

"Pretty smug, aren't you?" Canby said.

He stared at the ceiling. Lois fiddled at the desk. The Beatles were singing "Don't Let Me Down."

Suddenly Lois went to the bed and lay down, opening her arms voluptuously, twining Canby's hair in her fingers, smiling in exaggerated invitation.

"Hello there, brawn," she breathed sweetly.

"What?" Canby said. He burst out laughing, and they laughed together up to the smiling ceiling.

"You're adorable," Canby said. "I never thought you could be so adorable."

They kissed and were silent. They talked.

"I'm going to turn out the light," Canby said. "You can leave any time you want."

"I am going to leave," Lois said. "Not because I'm not perfectly happy but because I left my wallet with ninety dollars in the dorm where I ate dinner."

"Yeah," Canby said.

She got up.

"Can I call you again?"

"God, what a terrible question," Lois said. "That's just the way you're not supposed to think. Don't care about unreal things, it's—"

"Then why are you going off to look for your money?"

"Well, that's not the right way to think either. You can't disregard money, it's—"

"Money exists, the future doesn't. I know," said Canby.

"Right! Right! You're exactly right," Lois said. "Such a smart boy." She kissed him. "Aren't you going to walk me home to save me from rapists on the Common?"

Canby shrugged.

"Sure. Anything your little heart desires."

"You really don't have to walk me home," Lois said. "It's okay. And I should answer your question, though I don't really know how to answer it without abandoning my principles. It would be just as wrong for me not to answer it as it was for you to ask it. I'll just say that I don't have any desire for our—our relationship to be any—different, than it has been before. I mean, I love being with you as I love everything, but I don't think we should do anything to change the course of our lives."

"Fine," said Canby. "And good luck."

Through the closing door he heard her last words: ". . . terrific movie."

The Square was cold and deserted. Occasional neon lights threw hazy shapes of donkeys and horses into the wet sky. Lois walked with her hood up humming the only tune she could think of, "Gloria in excelsis Deo," timing breaths with steps.

As she came to the edge of the Common she was wondering why Canby had chosen 'outsider' for his example of a sign. Then he had thought of 'girl.'

She crossed the street, turning her neck to see past the edge of the hood. Her steps echoed on the glistening rain-wet pavement. A man was walking past her toward the Law School, a law student with a brief case under his arm. The sight of another night wanderer made her lonely. It was strange that being with people was often more lonely than being alone, she thought.

She passed through the gates of the Common, noting the trees sort of supplicating the sky and the big statue saying, like she had read, I hope I don't fall off this pedestal. There was a man at the base of the statue. He was wearing a white windbreaker and eying her.

"Uh-oh," Lois said aloud. She turned around and walked out the discretion gates and started up Garden Street is the better part of, still singing as she walked up the middle of the empty valor street. The man turned and started walking across the grass at an angle to her path. When he got to the edge he stopped and pretended to be looking at trees. She glanced at the empty hulk of Christ Church on her left. The red glow of the Sheraton Commander sign was smeared on its roof like streaming blood. She turned around and walked back to Massachusetts Avenue. She would walk all the way around to Shepard Street if she had to. There were still cars on Mass Ave.

She looked back for the man but couldn't see him. Her voice continued singing "Gloria" like a stuck needle, her steps echoed inside the blinkering hood. She decided she could chance Follett Street since the man was nowhere in sight. As she turned the corner she looked back and saw the man sitting on a bench far away in the middle of the Common, his jacket a spot of white in a web of dark shapes.

Lois watched her eyes burn in the mirror. She was too restless to read. She took a box of crayons and started pressing concentric circles onto a piece of paper: yellow, yellow orange, orange, orange red, red, purple in the center. Then she reversed the order: purple, red, red orange, orange, orange yellow, yellow. It looked like a gigantic sunburst. She tacked it onto the wall.

She brushed her hair and undressed. She got into bed. But she was too restless to sleep. She closed her eyes and saw a white spot in the darkness.

She got out of bed and picked up the telephone. She put a handkerchief over the receiver and dialed Canby's number.

"Hello," his sleepy voice said.

"Have an orgasm for me," she whispered crudely. She hung up, turned out the light, and got into bed.

LAS VEGAS TILT

LAWRENCE FERLINGHETTI

I
Past the highway sign that reads
            THE FATE OF THE WORLD
                    DEPENDS UPON
            THE WAY WE LIVE:
            SEE SOUTH SAN FRANCISCO
We're into the Big Sky
the whole earth catalog spread below
Day moon flies by
                    like a coin
                    flipped into Vegas
Banks of cloud
                    whir thru slots
                                of jetstream
        Ding-ding jackpots
                            flush up
                into blue air
Pilots up front
                with Southren accents
            in hidden cab
            pulling slotted levers

A tailwind helps us
                    thru a backward hour
          with vodka on the rock
Down down so soon
                    into Vegas
with fear & loathing
                    we drop ding-a-ling
          into it
Help Help
"We are beginning our gradual descent"
down Dante's fire escape
past friendly Bogey at five o'clock
Strike
      the dingbat zone
Tumblers spin
Landscape lights up
And the world registers TILT
We dip down
thru bumpy airpockets
banks of cloud-pinballs
Buffalo Heads
in silverdollar windtunnels
five-and-dime intestines
Touch down
jiggle down on rubber wheels
dolly up to it
in life's slick chariot
of the sun
Judas Iscariot
on the run

II
Spacecraft Earth spins on
And in the airport
the first slots light up
flashing on & off
                COIN ACCEPTED
          whir whir whir
                INSERT COIN

Indian Head rejects
>   fall out the Coin Return
where one-armed masturbators wait
Flushed out
>   we stagger into it
Landed in desert
>   we find no desert
no Nile to float down
>   with Voznesensky
but Cleopatra's Barge near Nero's Nook
>   with real plastic fish in its pool
>   plastic raft to float on
>   down Mississippis
>   A Moscow poet and an American on it

Where Tom Sawyer?
>   Who Huck Finn?
>   Where Injun Jim?

Jesus in dark glasses
on the bus to the Strip
carrying thirty pieces of silver
in a paper bag
In front of him an epileptic
in a gold golf cap
shaking his head continuously
uncontrollably
The silverhaired busdriver starts up
humming a tune from *Naughty Marietta*
We hum past

>   Tropicana Avenue   Lone Palm Motel
>   Shell Mobil   Private Pool Suites   Looney Tunes
> HEAVEN   Funny Farm   Rent-a-Car   Solarcaine
>   Paradise Road Blue Chip Stamps   GOLF
> Ice   Le Cafe   THE END   Drugs   HACIENDA
>   Mormon Temple   Towaway Zone   Coppertone
>   Gulf   Silver Slipper   Auto Refrigeration
>   Progressive Jackpots   Nevada Visitors Bureau
>   Penny Slots & Free Drinks   Las Vegas Boulevard
>   Play Nickels Win New Car   Hughes Air West
>   Bonanza Casino   Check Cashing Service

FOLIES BERGERE "Never Before"   Sage & Sand
Hunt Breakfast   HOOVER DAM
"Old-Fashioned Hospitality"
Frontier Hotel
LAS VEGAS HILTON
THE DUNES
STARDUST
Westward Ho
SHOWBOAT
FLAMINGO
DESERT INN
PYRAMIDS
CAESAR'S PALACE
Orange Julius
Our Marriage Chapel
Little Church of the West
"Thirty Dollar Weddings"
"Go Home Satisfied or Refund"

Jesus Christ Superstar gets off

"Everyman, I'll go with thee
and be thy guide
In thy most need to go
by thy side"

III
The end of the American dream
begins again
on the Street That Never Sleeps

And "the extraordinary adventure of white America"
roars on
amid the proofs it never experienced the Middle Ages
A huge cowboy on a hundred-foot horse
sits astride main street downtown
raises his neon Stetson
and says electronically
                    "Howdy, pardner"

His voice fills the air
       his voice is everywhere
       his picture printed in
          The Voice of the Rockies
       in the *Desert News*
         with his daily horoscope:
"Scorpions are mystery men, violent and volcanic inside, decep-
tively cool outside. They believe in revenge and vigorous pursuit
of women. The women among them make good spies, the men good
Mafia dons or police officers, either way, and superb athletes. Let
not Aries enter these premises."

Desert News sifts in like sand:
        CLEVELAND MAFIA RULES VEGAS
      "Geologists Say No Vegas Fault"
     "Hearst's Daughter Castigates Hearst's America
       Attacks 'Absolute Spiritual Bankcruptcy' "
"People change in Vegas and become what they would like
   to become and what they can't become back home"
        "Who Is Not on the Hustle
           In Life's Lottery?"
A covey of Oklahoma Mothers
with cowboy escorts
lands in The Blue Lagoon
A honeymoon couple from north Duluth
parks their blue Ford Phaeton
and struggles to the slots
Lady in lobby in powderblue pants & clogs
sprays her hair with a blue spray can
talking on a lobby phone
      "We come down here to a land sale.
      We dint buy no land
      but they give us free tickets
      to everything!"
A Japanese student with a skin problem
and a camera
scurries past to the john
An Indian with a skin problem
and a turban
is having trouble with his zipper

Slots whir in the Men's Room
          PRESS BUTTON TO FLUSH
And out come the coins or condoms
A minister in blue
with no skin condition
walks by jingling
a pocketful of dimes
Stands up to a slot
jiggles his pants
presses a button
and drowns

IV
                    ELECTRONIC SHOOTING GALLERY
               in the "Circus Circus":
             "Shoot the Red Dot"
          "You're in the heart
             of the deepest and darkest
                    jungles of Africa—
                Step up
                         to the shooting counter, hunters—
               pick up a gun, put a quarter in
                              the slot in front of you
                 and take careful aim—"
"All the animals you hit
      will scream, yell, move or holler—
Take your time
              and hit all the red dots—

"Come in, hunters,
          if you're brave enough to face
             the dangers of the jungle,
          pick up a gun
             put a quarter in the slot
                    and start shooting—

"A deadly jungle killer
                    the black python
          is hanging from a tree
             waiting for someone
                to make *the wrong move*—

"Watch the animals perform—
        Pick up a gun
            and let them have it—
                You get fifteen shots—

"On your left you see a native
            with a blowgun—
        When he's aiming at you
                        shoot him—

"You're in the heart
        of the deepest and darkest
                    jungles of Africa—"

KLEAN OUT KIKES
    KLEAN OUT WOPS
        KLEAN OUT REDSKINS
            KLEAN OUT SPICS
                KLEAN OUT CREEPS
                    KLEAN OUT FREAKS
                        KLEAN OUT BLACK TRASH
(GEORGE JACKSON LIVES)

            "There once was a man
            who sold the Lion's skin
            while the beast still lived
            and was killed
            while hunting him"

V
L'heure bleue
on the Strip
where time does not exist
except on the wrist of the dealer
and all that glisters is not gelt
and "behind the tinsel is the real tinsel"
in a Monopoly Game fantasy
dreamed up maybe by some Mormon Moloch
during the Great Depression

and stretched out there
in the great American desert
like some portable instant city
set down on the face of another planet
A five-mile long strip of gyzm
squeezed out like dry toothpaste on a cake

In desert dust storms
tumbleweeds
still blow
across Las Vegas Boulevard
and still will blow
after a river runs thru
Caesar's parkinglot
with its cargo of dead cars

The Strip lights up
like a pinball machine
or a linear accelerator
brighter than the moon up close
the sky a neon ceiling
for a room inside a lightbulb
where it does no good to close your eyes

A helicopter from the Stardust Casino
moves the stars about
over the Appian Way
And the Roman legions come rolling
like a Rose Bowl Parade
with Caesar's Great Triumphal Car
drawn by six Percherons
hung with elephant bells
and leading Dürer's Rhinoceros
on a string

There is a thrill in the air
The Roman legions come rolling
up to Caesar's Palace

Centurions
   swing off their horseless chariots
    parade up thru the gates
   come to a halt & raise their visors
    And look about
   The face of the pit boss stares out
    chewing the butt end
  of a burned-out Havana
He raises his right arm
      holds it like a salute
  and brings it down with a crash
     There is a whirring sound
      His eyes light up and spin
       with dollar signs in them

VI
Like a lost plane
    with feathered wings
The Winged Victory of Samothrace
  has landed somehow
   in front of
  CAESAR'S PALACE
built by building trades
  with union funds
       Martial's Palatine Sonnet
      quoted in the menu
     And "Room Service a Roman Feast"
     in the Frank Sinatra Suite
  but no food served with Harry Belafonte
  at the Midnight Supper Show
   designed precisely to disgorge
   the lushed-up masses
    directly into the
        carrousel Casino
  groaning with gaming tables
       Roulette Baccarat Keno
   in a sea of slotmachines
  one of which once in a while lights up
   shakes all over

showers out Caesar's own silverdollars
and emits a puff of smoke
Whiskey America plunges in
into the Soft Machine
into the steaming pits
as into a scene from Dante
painted by Gustave Doré
whose clouds were angels
Caesar not Virgil thy guide

Wearing blue and carrying a feather
will not win
Belafonte himself falls in
and drops $27,000
at baccarat
and next night sings a song-cry
about the pit bosses:
"If it moves and is warm
I will fleece it"

And all that glisters
is not guilt
at the baccarat tables
two dealers deal
the final Big Brother trip
And two pit bosses watch them
and three foremen watch the pit bosses
and one pit boss watches three foremen
from behind two-way mirrors
on the low ceiling
under which circulate the masses
mixed with house-dicks

Hoc in terra Caesar est

The pudgy pit boss squats
on his highchair throne
rings on fat fingers
and a fat cigar clutched loose
a De Mille Caesar
with lizard looks watching wrong moves

Drear players with coin-eyes
　　　　　stuck like horned toad zombies
　　　　　　round the board
"Phlebas the Phoenician a fortnight dead"
　　　holds his cards and hangs his head
Dawn breaks outside somewhere
　　　　　　　and the deal continues
Gold sun bursts forth unseen somewhere
　　　　　　　through a cottonwood grove
　　And the big shuffle goes on
The walls themselves fall down
　　　　　　as in Buster Keaton movies
　　and they still play on
　　　　Pale Faces turning paler
　　　　impaled on rotating spits in pits
　　　　roasted with rotating oranges
　　　　　　apples & cherries
　　　　　　　under glass
　　　　through which also wink & blink
　　　　Buffalo Heads & Indian Heads
in hock in terror　　　　　in base-relief
　　And Eisenhower eyes and Kennedy eyes
And the weird Third Eye that winks not
　　　from its Transamerica Pyramid
　　　　in the dollar's
　　　　　　　green desert
　　　　upon which hangs a sign
　　　　　　　　WE NEVER CLOSE

VII
And now at Angels Peak in morning light
thirty miles above Vegas
Andrei Voznesensky asks no quarter
but takes a coin of his own
and drops it in the mouth of the daughter
of the President of Caesar's Palace
and pulls her right arm down
and waits for the virgin coin
to fall out below
if he's that lucky

And at Indian Rock Refuge
we get out
and climb up the steep riprap
to the Indian cave at the top
from which the flat world can be seen
and drop small round flat stones
into slots in it

And await the final
deluge jackpot landslide
of earth and life

in which the fate of the world
depends upon
the way we live

November–December 1971

NOTES

I. "whole earth catalog spread below"–cf. *The Whole Earth Catalog,* published by the Portola Institute in Menlo Park, California, an ecology-oriented guide back to Earth.

"Southren"–dialect spelling, as pronounced, southeastern United States.

"fear & loathing"–cf. two-part feature in *Rolling Stone* (San Francisco, November 1971), "Fear & Loathing in Las Vegas."

II. "with Voznesensky"–The Russian poet came to the U.S.A. in October 1971, and read at Project Artaud in San Francisco on October 22, in an event sponsored by City Lights Books. I read the translations, and two or three weeks later flew to meet him in Las Vegas, where we read at the University of Nevada. Voznesensky spent a total of one month touring the U.S.A. before returning to the U.S.S.R.

"down Mississippis"–Actually it was Yevgeni Yevtushenko who in the summer of 1969 or '70 was rumored to be planning a trip down the Mississippi on a boat with John Updike. It never happened.

"carrying thirty pieces of silver"–cf. Judas Iscariot.

III. "the extraordinary adventure of white America"—cf. Jean
     Genet's introduction to *Soledad Brother: The Prison Letters
     of George Jackson* (New York: Bantam Books, 1970).

IV. The entire section in quotes is a verbatim transcription of the
     taped voice broadcast perpetually in the "Shooting Gallery."
     "KLEAN OUT KIKES" etc.—for related background, cf. *Sole-
     dad Brother*, page 195.

     "There once was a man/who sold the Lion's skin. . . ."—quoted
     by George Jackson in his *Soledad Brother*, page 19, from
     Rafael Sabatini's *The Lion Skin*. See also Jackson's castiga-
     tion of white capitalism, page 182: "Didn't it raise pigs and
     murder Vietnamese? Didn't it glut some and starve most of
     us? Didn't it build housing projects that resemble prisons
     and luxury hotels and apartments that resemble the Hang-
     ing Gardens on the same street? Didn't it erect a school and
     then open a whorehouse? Build an airplane to sell a tran-
     quilizer tablet? For every church didn't it construct a
     prison? For each new musical discovery didn't it produce
     as a by-product ten new biological warfare agents? Didn't
     it aggrandize men like Hunt and Hughes [of Las Vegas]
     . . . ?"

V.   "behind the tinsel is the real tinsel"—originally applied to Hol-
     lywood. From a remark by Oscar Levant.

     "Monopoly Game fantasy"—Both Las Vegas and the game
     Monopoly were invented out of cardboard in the thirties at
     the bottom of the Depression.

     "Caesar's parkinglot"—A river does run through the lot during
     the worst rainy season.

     "Caesar's Great Triumphal Car"—see the drawing by Albrecht
     Dürer.

VI. "Soft Machine"—see William S. Burroughs's book of that title
     (New York: Grove Press, 1966), the first part of which he
     must have written while looking at Hieronymous Bosch's
     paintings of "Inferno" and the "Garden of Delights."

     "a De Mille Caesar"—Cecil B. De Mille, Hollywood producer
     of "spectaculars" with "casts of thousands."

     "weird Third Eye"—see the back of the American dollar bill.

VII. These incidents in fact occurred while I was searching for
     symbolism which would syncretize the poem.

LOVE

CLARICE LISPECTOR

Translated by Giovanni Pontiero

Feeling a little tired, with her purchases bulging her new string bag, Anna boarded the tram. She placed the bag on her lap and the tram started off. Settling back in her seat she tried to find a comfortable position, with a sigh of mild satisfaction.

Anna had nice children, she reflected with certainty and pleasure. They were growing up, bathing themselves and misbehaving, they were demanding more and more of her time. The kitchen, after all, was spacious with its old stove which made explosive noises. The heat was oppressive in the apartment which they were paying off in instalments, and the wind, playing against the curtains which she had made herself, reminded her that if she wanted to she could pause to wipe her forehead, and contemplate the calm horizon. Like a farmer. She had planted the seeds which she held in her hand, no others, but only those. And they were growing into trees. Her brisk conversations with the electricity man were growing, the water filling the tank was growing, her children were growing, the table was growing with food, her husband arriving with the newspapers and smiling with hunger, the irritating singing of the maids resounding through the block. Anna tranquilly put her small, strong hand, her life, current to everything. Certain times of

78

the afternoon struck her as being critical. At a certain hour of the afternoon the trees that she had planted laughed at her. And when nothing more required her strength, she became anxious. Meanwhile she felt herself more solid than ever, her body had become a little thicker, and it was worth seeing the manner in which she cut out blouses for the children, the large scissors snapping into the material. All her vaguely artistic aspirations had for some time been channeled into making her days fulfilled and beautiful; with time her taste for the decorative had developed and supplanted intimate disorder. She seemed to have discovered that everything was capable of being perfected, that each thing could be given a harmonious appearance; life itself could be created by Man.

Deep down, Anna had always found it necessary to feel the firm roots of things. And this is what a home had surprisingly provided. Through tortuous paths, she had achieved a woman's destiny, with the surprise of conforming to it almost as if she had invented that destiny herself. The man whom she had married was a real man, the children she mothered were real children. Her previous youth now seemed alien to her, like one of life's illnesses. She had gradually emerged to discover that life could be lived without happiness: by abolishing it she had found a legion of persons, previously invisible, who lived as one works—with perseverance, persistence and contentment. What had happened to Anna before possessing a home of her own stood forever beyond her reach: that disturbing exaltation which she had often confused with unbearable happiness. In exchange she had created something ultimately comprehensible, the life of an adult. This was what she had wanted and chosen.

Her precautions were now reduced to alertness during the dangerous part of the afternoon, when the house was empty and she was no longer needed; when the sun reached its zenith, and each member of the family went about his separate duties. Looking at the polished furniture, she felt her heart contract a little with fear. But in her life there was no opportunity to cherish her fears—she suppressed them with that same ingenuity she had acquired from domestic struggles. Then she would go out shopping or take things to be mended, unobtrusively looking after her home and her family. When she returned it would already be late afternoon and the children back from school would absorb her attention. Until the evening descended with its quiet excitement. In the morning she would awaken surrounded by her calm domestic duties. She would find the furniture dusty and dirty once more, as if it had returned repentant. As for herself, she mysteriously formed part of the soft, dark roots of the earth. And anonymously she nourished life. It was pleasant like this. This was what she had wanted and chosen.

The tram swayed on its rails and turned into the main road. Suddenly the wind became more humid, announcing not only the passing of the afternoon but the end of that uncertain hour. Anna sighed with relief and a deep sense of acceptance gave her face an air of womanhood.

The tram would drag along and then suddenly jolt to a halt. As far as Humaita she could relax. Suddenly she saw the man stationary at the tram stop. The difference between him and others was that he was really stationary. He stood with his hands held out in front of him—blind.

But what else was there about him which made Anna sit up in distrust? Something disquieting was happening. Then she discovered what it was: the blind man was chewing gum . . . a blind man chewing gum. Anna still had time to reflect for a second that her brothers were coming to dinner—her heart pounding at regular intervals. Leaning forward, she studied the blind man intently, as one observes something incapable of returning our gaze. Relaxed, and with open eyes, he was chewing gum in the dwindling light. The facial movements of his chewing made him appear to smile then suddenly stop smiling, to smile and stop smiling. Anna stared at him as if he had insulted her. And anyone watching would have received the impression of a woman filled with hatred. She continued to stare at him, leaning more and more forward—until the tram gave a sudden jerk throwing her unexpectedly backward. The heavy string bag toppled from her lap and landed on the floor—Anna cried out, the conductor gave the signal to stop before realizing what was happening, and the tram came to an abrupt halt. The other passengers looked on in amazement. Too paralyzed to gather up her shopping, Anna sat upright, her face suddenly pale. An expression, long since forgotten, awkwardly reappeared, unexpected and inexplicable. The Negro newsboy smiled as he handed over her bundle. The eggs had broken in their newspaper wrapping. Yellow sticky yolks dripped between the strands of the bag. The blind man had interrupted his chewing and held out his unsteady hands, trying in vain to grasp what had happened. She removed the parcel of eggs from the string bag accompanied by the smiles of the passengers. A second signal from the conductor and the tram moved off with another jerk.

A few moments later people were no longer staring at her. The tram was rattling on the rails and the blind man chewing gum had remained behind for ever. But the damage had been done.

The string bag felt rough between her fingers, not soft and familiar as when she had knitted it. The bag had lost its meaning; to find herself on that tram was a broken thread; she did not know what to do with the purchases on her lap. Like some strange music, the world started up again around her. The damage had been done. But why? Had she forgotten that there were blind people? Compassion choked her. Anna's breathing became heavy. Even those things which had existed before the episode were now on the alert, more hostile, and even perishable. The world had once more become a nightmare. Several years fell away, the yellow yolks trickled. Exiled from her own days, it seemed to her that the people in the streets were vulnerable, that they barely maintained their equilibrium on the surface of the darkness—and for a moment they appeared to lack any sense of direction. The perception of an absence of law came so unexpectedly that Anna clutched the seat in front of her, as if she might fall off the tram, as if things might be overturned with the same calm they had possessed when order reigned.

What she called a crisis had come at last. And its sign was the intense pleasure with which she now looked at things, suffering and alarmed. The heat had become more oppressive, everything had gained new power and a stronger voice. In the Rua Voluntarios da Patria, revolution seemed imminent, the grids of the gutters were dry, the air dusty. A blind man chewing gum had plunged the world into a mysterious excitement. In every strong person there was a lack of compassion for the blind man, and their strength terrified her. Beside her sat a woman in blue with such an expression it made Anna avert her gaze rapidly. On the pavement a mother shook her little boy. Two lovers held hands smiling . . . And the blind man? Anna had lapsed into a mood of compassion which greatly distressed her.

She had skillfully pacified life; she had taken so much care to avoid upheavals. She cultivated an atmosphere of serene understanding separating each person from the others; her clothes were

clearly designed to be practical, and she could choose the evening's
film from the newspaper—and everything was done in such a man-
ner that each day should smoothly succeed the previous one. And
a blind man chewing gum was destroying all this. Through her
compassion Anna felt that life was filled to the brim with a sicken-
ing nausea.

Only then did she realize that she had passed her stop ages ago.
In her weak state everything touched her with alarm. She got off
the tram, her legs shaking, and looked around her, clutching the
string bag stained with egg. For a moment she was unable to get
her bearings. She seemed to have plunged into the middle of the
night.

It was a long road, with high yellow walls. Her heart beat with
fear as she tried in vain to recognize her surroundings; while the
life which she had discovered continued to pulsate and a gentler,
more mysterious wind caressed her face. She stood quietly observ-
ing the wall. At last she recognized it. Advancing a little further
alongside a hedge, she passed through the gates of the Botanical
Garden.

She strolled wearily up the central avenue, between the palm
trees. There was no one in the garden. She put her parcels down
on the ground and sat down on the bench of a side path where
she remained for some time.

The wilderness seemed to calm her, the silence regulating her
breathing and soothing her senses.

From afar she saw the avenue where the evening was round and
clear. But the shadows of the branches covered the side path.

Around her there were tranquil noises, the scent of trees, chance
encounters among the creeping plants. The entire garden frag-
mented by the ever more fleeting moments of the evening. From
whence came the drowsiness with which she was surrounded? As
if induced by the drone of birds and bees. Everything seemed
strange, much too gentle, much too great.

A gentle, familiar movement startled her and she turned round
rapidly. Nothing appeared to have stirred. But in the central lane
there stood immobile an enormous cat. Its fur was soft. With an-
other silent movement, it disappeared.

Agitated, she looked about her. The branches swayed, their
shadows wavering on the ground. A sparrow foraged in the soil.
And suddenly, in terror, she imagined that she had fallen into an

ambush. In the garden there was a secret activity in progress which she was beginning to penetrate.

On the trees, the fruits were black and sweet as honey. On the ground there lay dry fruit stones full of circumvolutions like small rotted cerebrums. The bench was stained with purple sap. With gentle persistence the waters murmured. On the tree trunk the luxurious feelers of parasites fastened themselves. The rawness of the world was peaceful. The murder was deep. And death was not what one had imagined.

As well as being imaginary, this was a world to be devoured with one's teeth, a world of voluminous dahlias and tulips. The trunks were pervaded by leafy parasites, their embrace soft and clinging. Like the resistance that precedes surrender, it was fascinating; the woman felt disgusted, and it was fascinating.

The trees were laden, and the world was so rich that it was rotting. When Anna reflected that there were children and grown men suffering hunger, the nausea reached her throat as if she were pregnant and abandoned. The moral of the garden was something different. Now that the blind man had guided her to it, she trembled on the threshold of a dark, fascinating world where monstrous water lilies floated. The small flowers scattered on the grass did not appear to be yellow or pink, but the color of inferior gold and scarlet. Their decay was profound, perfumed. But all these oppressive things she watched, her head surrounded by a swarm of insects, sent by the more refined life in the world. The breeze penetrated between the flowers. Anna imagined rather than felt its sweetened scent. The garden was so beautiful that she feared Hell.

It was almost night now and everything seemed replete and heavy; a squirrel leapt in the darkness. Under her feet the earth was soft. Anna inhaled its odor with delight. It was both fascinating and repulsive.

But when she remembered the children, before whom she now felt guilty, she straightened up with a cry of pain. She clutched the package, advanced through the dark side path, and reached the avenue. She was almost running, and she saw the garden all around her aloof and impersonal. She shook the locked gates, and went on shaking them, gripping the rough timber. The watchman appeared, alarmed at not having seen her.

Until she reached the entrance of the building, she seemed to be on the brink of disaster. She ran with the string bag to the elevator, her heart beating in her breast—what was happening? Her compassion for the blind man was as fierce as anguish but the world seemed hers, dirty, perishable, hers. She opened the door of her flat. The room was large, square, the polished knobs were shining, the windowpanes were shining, the lamp shone brightly—what new land was this? And for a moment that wholesome life which she had led until today seemed morally crazy. The little boy who came running up to embrace her was a creature with long legs and a face resembling her own. She pressed him firmly to her in anxiety and fear. Trembling, she protected herself. Life was vulnerable. She loved the world, she loved all things created, she loved with loathing. In the same way as she had always been fascinated by oysters, with that vague sentiment of revulsion which the approach of truth provoked, admonishing her. She embraced her son, almost hurting him. Almost as if she knew of some evil—the blind man or the beautiful Botanical Garden—she was clinging to him, to him whom she loved above all things. She had been touched by the demon of faith. "Life is horrible," she said to him in a low voice, as if famished. What would she do if she answered the blind man's call? She would go alone . . . There were poor and rich places that needed her. She needed them . . . "I am afraid," she said. She felt the delicate ribs of the child between her arms, she heard his frightened weeping. "Mummy," the child called. She held him away from her, she studied his face and her heart shrank. "Don't let Mummy forget you," she said. No sooner had the child felt her embrace weaken than he escaped and ran to the door of the room, from where he watched her more safely. It was the worst look that she had ever received. The blood rose hot to her cheeks.

She sank into a chair, with her fingers still clasping the string bag. What was she ashamed of? There was no way of escaping. The very crust of the days which she had forged had broken and the water was escaping. She stood before the oyster. And there was no way of averting her gaze. What was she ashamed of? Certainly it was no longer pity, it was more than pity: her heart had filled with the worst will to live.

She no longer knew if she was on the side of the blind man or of the thick plants. The man little by little had moved away and in her torment she appeared to have passed over to the side of those who had injured his eyes. The Botanical Garden, tranquil and high, had been a revelation. With horror, she discovered that she belonged to the strong part of the world and what name should she give to her fierce compassion? Would she be obliged to kiss the leper, since she would never be just a sister? "A blind man has drawn me to the worst of myself," she thought, amazed. She felt herself banished because no pauper would drink water from her burning hands. Ah! it was easier to be a saint than a person! Good heavens, then was it not real that pity which had fathomed the deepest waters in her heart? But it was the compassion of a lion.

Humiliated, she knew that the blind man would prefer a poorer love. And, trembling, she also knew why. The life of the Botanical Garden summoned her as a werewolf is summoned by the moonlight. "Oh! but she loved the blind man," she thought with tears in her eyes. Meanwhile it was not with this sentiment that she would go to church. "I am frightened," she whispered alone in the room. She got up and went to the kitchen to help the maid prepare the dinner.

But life made her shiver like the cold of winter. She heard the school bell pealing, distant and constant. The small horror of the dust gathering in threads around the bottom of the stove, where she had discovered a small spider. Lifting a vase to change the water—there was the horror of the flower submitting itself, languid and loathsome, to her hands. The same secret activity was going on here in the kitchen. Near the waste bin, she crushed an ant with her foot. The small murder of the ant. Its minute body trembled. Drops of water fell on the stagnant water in the pool.

The summer beetles. The horror of those expressionless beetles. All around there was a silent, slow, insistent life. Horror upon horror. She went from one side of the kitchen to the other, cutting the steaks, mixing the cream. Circling around her head, around the light, the flies of a warm summer's evening. A night in which compassion was as crude as false love. Sweat trickled between her breasts. Faith broke her; the heat of the oven burned in her eyes.

Then her husband arrived, followed by her brothers and their wives, and her brothers' children.

They dined with all the windows open, on the ninth floor. An airplane shuddered menacingly in the heat of the sky. Although she had used few eggs, the dinner was good. The children stayed up, playing on the carpet with their cousins. It was summer and it would be useless to force them to go to sleep. Anna was a little pale and laughed gently with the others.

After dinner, the first cool breeze finally entered the room. The family were seated round the table. Tired after their day, happy in the absence of any discord, eager not to find fault. They laughed at everything, with warmth and humanity. The children grew up admirably around them. Anna took the moment like a butterfly, between her fingers before it might escape for ever.

Later, when they had all left and the children were in bed, she was just a woman looking out of the window. The city was asleep and warm. Would the experience unleashed by the blind man fill her days? How many years would it take before growing old again? The slightest movement on her part and she would trample one of her children. But with the ill will of a lover, she seemed to accept that the fly would emerge from the flower, and the giant water lilies would float in the darkness of the lake. The blind man was hanging among the fruits of the Botanical Garden.

What if that were the stove exploding with the fire spreading through the house, she thought to herself as she ran to the kitchen where she found her husband in front of the spilt coffee.

—"What happened?" she cried, shaking from head to foot. He was taken aback by his wife's alarm. And suddenly understanding, he laughed.

—"It was nothing," he said. "I am just a clumsy fellow." He looked tired, with dark circles under his eyes.

But, confronted by the strange expression on Anna's face, he studied her more closely. Then he drew her to him in a sudden caress.

—"I don't want anything ever to happen to you!" she said.

—"You can't prevent the stove from having its little explosions," he replied, smiling. She remained limp in his arms. This afternoon, something tranquil had exploded, and in the house everything struck a tragicomic note.

—"It's time to go to bed," he said, "it's late." In a gesture which was not his, but which seemed natural, he held his wife's hand, taking her with him, without looking back, removing her from the danger of living.

The giddiness of compassion had spent itself. And if she had crossed love and its hell, she was now combing her hair before the mirror, without any world for the moment in her heart. Before getting into bed, as if she were snuffing a candle, she blew out that day's tiny flame.

SIX POEMS

E. W. JOHNSON

THE CHASE

He seeks a guru
It will happen
This way:
In a room
Sitting on the floor, perhaps
Quite probably tripped
And someone will say
"I know
Why
You are here."
"Good."
He will answer
"Tell me."
His guru exists
Somewhere
But may be hiding.
Or maybe there's no guru
No reason
For being
In any room
Nowhere he must go
And no one who is
More informed
Than he.

WORDLESS

Giving away everything
That had taken years
To collect
With care
I emptied my house.
Before driving away
You hung a mandala
From my inside mirror
Sturdy
Made it yourself
On an acid trip
From wire and shaved sticks
Which traveled with me
Symbol
Of a love I'd have
With her
And didn't.
One year now
And you've never asked
Or known
Where or why it went
Or even that its memory
Still remains with me.

HOME VISIT

Reacting
To rules laid down
In childhood.
My old room
A stranger—
No friends
Left in town.
They call me Eddie.

But at night
I drink coffee
In their kitchen
Smoke some grass
Feed bits of sandwich
To my dog.
With them—
It's as if
I'd never been anywhere.

DESIGN

Tonight I watched
A television show
Where the hero
Threw the heroine
Onto her bed.
Afterward, they both seemed
Satisfied.
Not like you
And me
Who wonder
At what we exchanged.
Or didn't . . .
But I just couldn't play
Hero-seducer
Where everything matched
And was perfect
Your apartment
So carefully arranged
That
Somehow
There wasn't room for me.

SELF-PORTRAIT WITH CIGAR

I am a nasty
Cribbage player—
A billboard claim
That I can beat
Anybody.
Proving this
Upon demand.
Often vicious
With the craft
Of writing
I use my talent
As a club.
Joint-rolling
Too
Holds a certain
Formal
Aggression
Alas—
I do
So few things
Well.

EDUCATION

I would like to explain to my children
What to expect
From an indifferent
Perhaps even hostile
World
So that they might know
As little pain
As possible
By avoiding the traps
Their father
Unwisely
Fell victim to
But if I do this
I must also explain
That those traps
Were the most vital moments
Of their father's life.

ELEVEN POEMS FROM *HOME*

TOBY OLSON

1
I had wanted to tell you something
about our lives
and what we do together:

a large thing
I have forgotten

many times
I have learned it again:

it is a lesson therefore
the times are hard
sometimes

when we are together
I feel I could write you a letter about its
lacking necessity

in what is already
complete, I

would like to tell you about it
I have forgotten
what it was.

2
It could surely become more involved: we'd
say things about structure

the sexual possibilities
of every flat surface in the house

and the round surfaces also
and the pointed ones: all

the possible pleasures of invention.
There are new objects constantly:

this week
a table and a chest

We walk out in our new coats:
we become more involved with each other.

3
Outside the wind is serious
that which enters
the cracked window
is tentative. we believe that
we have controlled something
tangible. in our lives, we say
we live in the eye
of a hurricane.
                    down
bay-side, the wind is furious.
unaccountably: the ocean
is flat and calm: at the same time
in our lives, we say
hard things to one another: hate
and then we love each other:
out, at the Cape's end
it comes together.

4
That which goes over the land is valuable:
the golden hemorrhoids in the Ark

of the Covenant — Jesus
it's so easy to say these things

of the spirit coming from the asses of people:
the simple truth

is my sustenance comes from your body
I am kept alive

by it
I travel over the land:

lustful
for its value.

5
Sometimes, when we have spoken,
you have carried those things with you,
however foolish: to work
in the lunch room — I have

   taken them too: the specific
touch of your nipple, whatever woman
I talk to, and you

are doing the same
with the men: we

enter the conversation
together.

6

This one is awkward, because
it is written in need: the earth breaks
open, painful, trees come
into existence

It is all simple
it happens — this
does not happen
is written

abstracted — possibly
the head breaks
too:

    the first wife
Crab-Woman   Beautiful
Cripple

        This is addressed to. . .

need:
to have said *get a cane*! can't
drive a shift car
I had one

        Crutch
for the crab, walking
whatever vector   I'm

not a simple man
this is awkward, painful
to say it: the earth breaks

      the head breaks open

      this is addressed to
      Annie   Crab-Wife
Beautiful-Cripple,

and Miriam
we live here—
make plans.

7
Love—
that I have not spoken your name
and yet it comes to me
on the sand at Longnook   seeing
the boy walking
                    along the beach from P-Town . that
I should be doing this
one morning
                early   before the sun
breaks on the forearm   Leave you
in bed   park at the lighthouse   then
go along that beach   no shells
or driftwood   only
that bright tower and light
behind me
            brings me
over the same ground   quicker
knowing
you are awake
await me
Miriam—

8
The fact
occurring in some light
is the beauty of its existence.

it could be a light in the eyes,
as passage
            into another life:
those things
not left behind
unless, they are not spoken.

or maybe the light in garments
a wife leaves around the house,
each specific gesture
seen in the light of her absence.

If I take you
into this poem
it is not casual:

in closed rooms, tho
some light present
we
    have looked at each other,

understand:
        fulfillment
I am not speaking of messages;
occurrence
        whatever the light
is its own justice.

The rules
we get from the earth
    are simple:
behave yourself, do good deeds,
live in your body,
beware
that you love each other,
be honest about it.

Barbara: here in this room
writing this poem for you
I am somehow
warned away from myself
into some different magnitude: it's Fall

the earth
lays waste,
        a ringed-necked pheasant
is passing out of the bushes.
the way
we say he ignores us
not thought
        as we understand it, but
his own life in the balance
we call it) of nature.
he walks in a failing light.

What I am saying
is not matter
        of convention.
we both know people
throwing their lives away
on forms
        And I too
have probably done so.

        that's why
I am not full of understanding,

or able to speak
clearly
        about what I think
of love.

A gentleman turns to a lady.
it is a matter of convention,
        earth
breaks open:

        Fall
the ringed-necked pheasant
is dead in his tracks
when the hunters come, tho
they walk in a different light
and are so clearly
awkward,

        as I am too
remembering
the light of your cow-eyes,
though they seem now
less domestic.

Do not think of psychology.
Is it so hard to accept?

It is.

    complications,
things blurred in a bright light
of occurrence,

a human light.
For me
the earth breaks open
again,
       a new pheasant,
in-
distinguishable,
comes out of the bushes.
and walks on the earth again.

the light softens
around his clarity.

9
That which is tangible is a blessing
or does not enter as question:
   I'm sorry; will you accept that?
What kind of day did you have?

or else dinner and more talk.
and that's fine, too:
   each day, a new
illusion supplanted: information
vague information.

. . . who loosens her bra
in the bright light of the bedroom:

aureole . aureole

10

It is not that we think
          less of each other,
we expect too much
of ourselves. sometimes
wrong things

things fostered, those
coming forth thru passion,
memory, belief
                    in the way we feel
we live in the world

wrong-headed.

it is brutal: this week
how many times have I touched you?
I mean, passing
                    by you. locked
in our own image
we think changing
tomorrow
          's thought of some new alteration
of passion. memory

rage at wanting to speak
and then be done with it.

The world changes
constantly
                    and memory too
and yet
what is constant is distance, tho
that is what brought us together

Miriam, there is no
depth of feeling in these words, but only
the lack of it
                    We become
the things we despise
because we are close enough
to hate them

rage
in their constant distance
from us

Home
changes

it is brutal:
the various houses shake
me, back into other places

of which I cannot feel
or talk about with sense,
and yet they have brought us together.

—nor have you spoken to me
in a long time

I'm writing, you're
reading:
it is a condition of life
we live together

It's not
that we think less of each other
or that it never happens

it seems
for a long time
I have not touched you,

nor have I touched myself.

11
Facts:
become hard things to define

I mean brute facts:
a knife when it cuts

the fact of love
All these times

I have tried to get it said:
the cat pushing the mohair throw

brute fact
of a world full of resemblances:

your eyes your
body

smell of your body:
cuts.

BROKENNOSEJOB

MIA RAFFEL

To Cecilio García-Camarillo
who likes things that are made out of bamboo

1
Under the ribs of this hyena. I wonder how I got to be his heart?
I get a craving for things I ate, saw, licked, held, or wore, when I
too was a beast.
I hit the hyena fifty times a minute but he never cries. He whines
& bays at the sun, I flay his ribs until I faint, but he never cries. He
thinks insects are nervous turds; night, a sheet of snakes; and only
eats stones & carrion teeth. With these he grows a new set of toe-
nails every afternoon. And to that end I am obliged to pray.
I get a craving for things I ate, saw, licked, held, or wore, when I
too was a beast.

> Lemons
> Warmth
> Seeds
> Fire
> Sound

and once I saw a red bird
eating a lichee nut.

2

Shelled suddenly in the left elbow, I ran for the hippopotamus river. I kick the hippopotamus that sips at my wound. Remembering my little children, I cry; bleeding, it's my ribs that were shelled. The hippopotamus that eats my ribs eats them slowly one at a time. I put 3 fingers to hold up my lungs. Cryingcalling my little children, I hold them to my throat. And that sustains my life four minutes & a few seconds longer.

3

After a late breakfast, my mynah bird vomited a plate of bubbles & a pickle fork. He lay down; I stroked his head. Licking a little blue scruff off his wing, 'What the hell kind of a morning is this for singing?' he said. I smiled, but he turned his face to the wall. 'They're rough,' he said, '—mornings.'

4

This piano is syphilitic. As I started to play, scabby sores from my thumbs stuck between A and B-flat. 'The notes are stuck!' screamed an inmate. I extricated my thumbs and went on without comment. Better this than silence.

5

When the plumbing was defective I pissed in a cup. The hotness of that. When I had nothing to eat I picked, scraped, scoured, and boiled dandelion greens. The pill bugs I boiled separately. When I ran out of fire & water I had to warm the dandelion greens and the pill bugs with the cup of hot urine. I tried to get a reading on my misery from the sky. But there were no clouds in the sky that year.

6

An armadillo is not a friendly creature. When I put out my scaly hand, it spat on me. I gave it my dinner and it danced in the gravy. It searched for an exit, shivering. The sound of its shivering was conclusive. But left without even an armadillo I cried; and before it went the armadillo ate my tears.

7

The roof of the house was lowered to fit Uncle Jaime. 'I don't need all this space any more,' he croaked. They lowered it to his shoulders, to his waist, and at his request, to his knees. 'From here I can conduct my business,' he said, and stretching out smoothing his boots, he took out his purple harmonica.

8

I peeled a coconut. Then I ate the rind. 'It is this way that I want you to peel me and eat the rind,' I said.

9

Nose job. I mutter Zen parables. When the hammer strikes my face, only a rock garden is left above my mouth.

10

In the gas chamber I did not try to crawl the walls. I tried to tear my hands from my wrists so that they, my favorite part of myself, might die by my own wish.

11

'Eat this candy,' said the sailor, pleadingsugarstick. In his eyes wishes were simmering. A cowlicky boy, not yet warned by his mother against sugarstick, got into the sailor's car. Later the sailor laid him in a flannel blanket, asleep, near the school. A tattoo running from the boy's shoulder joint to his wrist: 'Capitol Junk Yard.' . . . 'Eat this candy,' mumbled the sailor another time, whisperingsugarstick. In his eyes wishes were embers. The croppedhair girl, towhead, littlemouthed, not yet warned against sugarstick, got into his car. Later the sailor laid her in the flannel blanket, waiting for the tattoo to cool.

12

Ferns will grow if they get water, will cover a wall & 2 white windows. The silver metal moon is a talisman. Is it for me?

13

The baby's fingers as she shysmiles turn back toward her mouth. Her hair is slippery and frail. She said to my friend, 'You have golden hands.' At that moment his hands melted Mexican evanescent gold, and he laughed.

14

Beadstrings I break my nails to fit a necklace for my babies. Flowers I will make them. I ignite patience on a stone urn: their incense.

15

Anna lay in her room spitglopping, 'Mehmeh,' goatmoan. She refused to sleep at night, so they take away her mattress in the day. Spit in matted auburn hair, white eyes, babymouth Anna. 'Anna,' I said her name. I touched her arm. 'It will be better. It will be better, Anna.' 'Fuck off, you whore,' she answered, kicking both my ankles.

16

20 blue, 2 red, 1 yellow, 2 red, 20 blue. Weave blanket of indifference. To get through coyote-scream night. 2 red, 1 yellow, 2 red. I had a turquoise ring once. A man who hated me threw it in the ocean. Bind my hair, weave my blind, hold my heart, 20 blue, 2 red, 20 blue.

17

A mystical-literary inmate called Sappho, who carried a brief case strapped to her back, asked me to tea. She gently stroked my breasts. 'Please,' I said, 'don't do that.' 'Then what would you like?' 'Read me a poem,' I said. She turned sharply away. 'I don't write poems. These are race track scores.'

18

Buttermilk is cowslip, adder weed, curd soup. I drink it when my blood faints. I dreamed that a country Indian girl who wore bracelets on her toes spent many hours every day making buttermilk for her husband, a yogi known for his snake-black goats, & the evening flute by which he called them to sleep.

19

I was standing by the shore when a whale imploded. Seeing that his teeth were still chattering, I said, 'Can I do anything?' 'Do it to a machine,' the teeth said. They scuttled away to the water, empowered with a new and unattractive intention.

20

14-yr.-old speedfreak Lisa ran to Anna with an unfolded secret in her hand. Attached to the hand was her arm, attached to the arm was a sling. 'Anna, lookit, I fell, Anna, listen.' Anna chewed black bread. 'Anna, you gotta listen, I fell down 2 flights of steps,' Lisa yelled. Anna spreads hospital margarine on black bread. 'Lookit this, *look*, for Christ's sake. I *broke* it!' Anna lifted her mouth. Her throat rolled back slowly, the lips lifting slowly, a murmur murmuring slowly into an overt exclamation: 'Huhuhahaha*ha*.' The eyes glinting hoarse maniac pleasure. She returns to her bread.

21

In the hours it took the sun to rise, I cowered, moldery cave, covered with spiders & glue, weeping. But never let the spiders hear that. I sang 'Ha Tikva,' the song older than the Jews, older than a sea gone marsh. Rocking on my heels, pulling the spikes from the backs of my knees. Ears broken, throat ripped, backs of knees black,
     'Ha Tikva,' 'Ha Tikva,' 'Ha Tikva.'
     'Ha Tikva.'

22

Old stickwrist Jimmy, you built yourself a tin house so you could hear the rain on the roof. The rain reminded you of lovemaking, so you fucked the drainpipe. Your cock has been sore ever since. And now that they won't give you whisky any more, you've given birth to a birdy cackle that is your greeting to men, your call of pain, & your memory of wild, drum-rattle rain.

23

Bina cradled all her babies at once during an asthma nightmare. When she fell out of bed their skulls cracked. 'They were all I ever had!' she screamed. The youngest smiled wryly as it departed from this world. 'Might try getting a self,' he chirped.

24

One of the doctors vomited on his notes. 'Jesus God,' he sobbed, 'now I'll never know whether she was defensive or offensive.' I offered him a betel nut, which he graciously accepted. 'You know,' he said, 'I always wanted to be a baseball player, but my dad wanted me to be a baseball player, so I went to med school.' I gave him another betel nut. He smiled shyly. 'Would you happen to have a cigarette or a jelly bean?'

25

My liver showed circular on the X-ray, so they took it out. My pancreas had a blue border around it, so they took it out. When I smiled you could notice a thin circle of tears, so they cut out my smile. Now I'm three-holed, & cold.

26

He had the honor of riding to his first sales conference in the new country in a blue tramcar. But he had to get off to urinate. In the kiosk the booths were furnished with shallow copper pans. A short man in a green vinyl uniform measured his urine & charged him accordingly. 'You can't!' he shouted, he was an important business-man, & he showed them his papers. But they later used the in-formation to attach his salary. They say he is now one of the most successful emigrants of the decade; but that his wife has left him since he became a compulsive bed-wetter.

27

'How did you feel when you took the 38 sleeping pills?' 'Nervous.' 'How did you feel when you woke up still alive?' 'Nervous.' I think of her trussed in an oxygen mask, armbands, and intravenous tubes. 'I wasn't depressed,' she said. 'I wasn't depressed when I did it, I'm not depressed now.' I looked at her stooped back, then embraced it. 'Does that feel better?' I asked. 'I don't know,' she said. 'It feels like a blanket.' 'A blanket?' 'I want to die wrapped in a blanket. You hold me, then I'll die wrapped in a blanket.'

28

Cottage cheese, pickled apples, and olives are the only edible food I've discovered in this hospital. I look at the serving-women: square elbows, mudeyes, metalmouthed, they hardly hear my requests whispered over the counter; but I urgently want to inform them before it is too late for them: cottage cheese, pickled apples, and olives.

29
Jeanne is getting a divorce for her birthday. Her hair reminds me
of chick-peas. & she seems to spit out chick-peas when she talks.
'He's in Vietnam. . . I dream they shoot his heart out. . . I dream
he begs me to take him back. . . I dream of his helmet, I dream he
aims his gun at my eyes. . . I dream I still love him. I love, I love
him.' And her eyes go thorns.

30
You gave me a rose. I gave you a silk screen. You gave me a bamboo
flute. I gave you a carved box. You gave me a rum cigar. I gave
you a Siamese monkey. You went for a walk on a hill, and didn't
return; but I know where you are. Can I give you a blackberry
branch without waiting for yours?

31
A white gazelle lay dying in a clearing. Beside it was a fuzzy orange
fawn. 'Go to the evergreen trees,' said the white gazelle. 'And ask
them. . .' Suddenly it died. The fawn ran, stricken, from its mother,
to the evergreen trees. 'Tell me,' it pleaded, 'what it was.' 'Little
fawn,' they whispered, 'a forest fire is coming, go back to your
mother.' It lay with its throat pressed against her ear, dreaming of
sweet milk, until consumed by impersonal flames.

32
359,862 automobiles ran over 84 skunks on the road to El Paso
this morning. The stench was alarming. Ladies covered their faces
with perfumed doilies. Men smoked asphalt-flavored cigars. A little
lunatic boy who escaped from here yesterday tried to read a funeral
service in the road, but a man from Dallas ran him down. Ques-
tioned by police, the man fingered his asphalt cigar. 'Danged
shame,' he mourned. 'Ah thought he was a skunk.'

33
The woman's black silk dress didn't quite fit, but a red brooch
clasped tightly between her breasts made it fit better. The silk
rustled, humming 'Floosh, floosh,' as the chair rocked; a great heavy
deal rocking chair in which she had nursed eight children, five of
whom had lived. The chair said, 'Careen, ech. Careen, ech.' Clock
ticking on the plaster mantel, listening to the silk, to the chair.

The woman was looking at her baby in its cradle. He was dressed like a good Danish Christian baby, but there was something Viking in him that disturbed her. From the neck down he was a white embroidered gown so long it bunched under the blankets; the soft ruddy fists were gentle in sleep; and a tiny golden cross lay neatly over his breast. She touched the cross with her hand, not a young nor soft hand, but one that had implemented much in the cause of life. The cross lay still. But the baby frowned in his sleep.

He was a dark-skinned baby with powerful limbs and a strange grown-up face. He had white eyebrows that stood in a straight line on his face. His white hair flew out in a circular bush around his head. His name was Valdemar, and he had a devilish will. But his will was not for himself. He wanted to *know* everything. When his cradle was under the trees he seemed to be counting their branches on his fingers. He stared at the clouds and clapped his hands, and laughed; or sometimes a cloud whose shape appeared like the others made him cry with fright. Apart from this he never cried. It was his eyes that worried his mother. They were grey—eagle-grey, sea-grey. The eyes of a fighter. The mother rested her foot on the cradle and made it rock. 'Loop-loop-loop-loop.' Silk, ticking, careen, rock. The cross on his breast. Thank God his eyes are closed. Sleep, Valdemar. He sleeps. She sings the lullaby her mother taught her: 'Sleep sweetly, sleep softly,' 'Sov sodelig, sov blodelig.' Valdemar's mouth moves in his sleep; he opens his eyes. The mother sings, silk, ticking, rocking, softly, sweetly, even the cross on his breast rests in the heart of the room. When the mother is finished, the child stirs restlessly. He wants the song again. Perhaps it will tame him. The mother laughs hopefully in her strong voice. She sings, and she rocks; rustling, she sings.

But the song did not tame him. As a young boy, Valdemar went out to war, and was sent home because those Viking eyes of his could not see far enough. His man's heart broke. He went to America, still a boy, apprenticed himself to a baker, worked hard each day, and fell passionately in love with a shy sensuous girl with wild brown eyes. He married her. He sired five children by her, the sixth died. Only one had Viking blood.

Valdemar now had thirty bakeries, servants, and a grandfather clock. But he had lost his Viking ship. He contracted a dangerous illness which he gave to his wife, and the Viking child was born with rickets, enlarged ribs, weak eyes, and a faint sweet smile. It lived. But Valdemar's heart died. He conducted his life with dignity and honor, but only one thing gave him peace. That was his mother's song, the one she had sung by his cradle; 'Sov sodelig, sov blodelig.' He selected a grandchild with bright eyes and slowly tried to teach her to play it on the piano. He was now an old man, blinded by cataracts, tone-deaf; but this one song he could make out.

He died before I, the grandchild, the Viking child's daughter, had learned the song. I can play it now. I play it for my son. It may be that he too is a Viking. But there is something else I have to say. When my grandfather Valdemar was a boy of four or five, he loved to play with sticks & grasshoppers near the windmill on his father's estate. He never went far from the field hands, because their work excited him. One night at sundown the men laid down their tools, wiping their necks with their bright handkerchiefs, and as they turned to go in and the cows were called, Valdemar started up. His eyes flamed, his face went dark with a sudden yearning, and a sound like that of a heron or a sea gull came from his throat. The men looked at him. Valdemar threw down his coat and ran fast, fast like a white four-legged thing with a white bush for a head, toward the horizon. 'Little one. Where are you going?' the men laughed. Valdemar ran, a sob caught in his throat, but he swallowed it. His eyes were fixed on the sky.

'Then where are you going?' called the men.

'To catch the sun!' he cried.

This and his song remain.

34

When you cry your eyelashes are thin bits of board. I smoothed your temples with my palms, waiting for your eyelashes to soften, & though you went on crying, they did. Your tears fell onto your hair and your mouth went small and hard. I put my arms around you and your mouth was younger. At last there were only the tears in your hair, and I watched them, sitting very still, until they dried.

35

Two old men went down to the river at midnight. There they climbed an olive tree and lit a candle. They talked until 4:30 about

wines, miracles, astrology, hangnails, soccer, arthritis, and erotic
Hindu rites. Then they got down and threw pebbles into the river
until dawn. They ate a small breakfast of figs & brandy and went
to sleep on the sand until late afternoon. Getting up, they shook
hands and went one to his village, the other to his mountain cave
at the edge of an orchard.

36

Once, I would like to feed a nightingale. I would give it chicken
soup with dumplings, rhubarb sauce, carrots cut in curls with
lemon and brown sugar, eggs in black butter, and grapes with sour
cream. Why, you may ask, would a nightingale eat this? Because
there is a Persian rug in a certain museum, in which I have seen
3 nightingales eating a broth with little circles, a red mound, soft
curls of orange, white circles enclosing yellow circles with brown
rims, & green circles glazed with white. The nightingales on the
rug were fed in turns by a parrot, and this service, too, I would
be honored to perform.
Since I was once in the Old Testament desert, I would also like to
return, waiting for a few days beside the mercury-glistening, evil
Dead Sea, until a crazy old prophet came out of a Gnostic tomb.
I would wash the sand off his body with my hair, and anoint his
head with persimmon juice. I would paint his toenails and his ear-
lobes blue, then build him a wooden throne facing away from the
sea. When he felt calm he would tell me the destruction of the
great temples, and I would write them on parchment. When he
was done, I would teach him to play the dulcimer, and his heart
eased, he would carry it back to sleep in his Gnostic grave.
Nightingales and prophets were respected once. Sometimes when
I am watching the moon, which opens & heals my body if I watch
with tenderness, I long, and I wait, for prophets and for nightin-
gales.

37

As the queen boarded her burial ship, the king & courtiers sobbed
hoarsely. She waved and called over her shoulder, 'Get ready now,
I'll be pulling off.' It was her whim to sail away in a burial ship,
because she had consumption. The people sobbed, coughed, sput-
tered, and she smiled dimly. When the boat had sailed an hour,
she stood up and danced on the prow. She had a little harpoon,

four Trollope novels, and a rubber tree in a dish. Forty years later
the Trollope novels wore out their bindings, but she harpooned
fish at dawn and at evening, and the rubber tree had grown to be
a forty-foot mast on the boat. Once a year she wrote a letter on a
rubber tree leaf with her fingernail and mailed it on the water. For
the rest, she invented a new art form, a boat dance with arched
feet, long swoops of the shoulders, and little dips and jumps; and
lived to be a hundred and eighty-eight.

38

Gary, a hospital attendant, muscular; television surfboard ad. I
wonder why. He once lived in Bolivia. 'What were the people like?'
'Oh, I don't know really.' 'Well what did you do there?' Blank
purple eyes. 'Not much.' 'How did you spend your time?' 'Oh, I
flew in my dad's plane a hundred or so times.' 'What else?' 'Took
a couple of jungle trips.' 'Tell me about one.' 'Oh, we canoed a
coupla miles into the jungle; the guides were tellin' us the last
white party was messed up by a bunch of head-hunters.' 'Man,
you knew you were going into that & you did it?' 'Hell, I was 16,
I was havin' a good time. We made camp, these 2 head-hunters
came up.' 'How did you know they were friendly?' 'Cause they
didn't put a 8-foot spear through our backs.' 'Oh. Go on.' 'One of
'em looks ninety, he's about 32. The guides talk to 'em in national
dialect. The other one, he looks about 30, he's 16, my age. We're
settin' up huts & a boa constrictor comes into one of 'em.' 'God,
what'd you do?' 'What d'you think? Killed it.' 'With a what?
Hatchet?' 'No no. Shotgun. Fast & easy. Then we skinned 'im &
cooked 'im up for dinner. The head-hunters ate with us. After a
while the old guys decided to turn in, but me & the young guy
wasn't tired at all. We wanted to go out & get something. So we
got in the canoe with our harpoons to go for some catfish—big
ones, 10 feet.' 'You'd done this before' 'Huh-uh. But I figure every
dude in the party's done it, & they all had a first time. They say
stick your fish & sit down real tight so's you don't get jerked out.
While we're scannin' around, I shine my flashlight on the shore &
there's 100 pairs of yellow eyes shinin' like marbles. I say to the
guy in Spanish, "What's that?" "Alligators." So I decided I didn't
want to fall out of the canoe that night.'
They go back to shore. Rolling in mud to screen themselves against
mosquitoes as long as their thumbs. They meet wild boar tracks.

Excited again, they follow them. But after some time they find their own trail, they've doubled around. Fresh tracks show a puma is stalking them. 'He might just as well not of eaten us as eaten us, he was probably lookin' for the boar. I mean, he knew we were a warm-blooded somethin' to eat, but he probably never smelled a human before, so he wanted to keep an eye on us. So we gave up & went to sleep.' Asleep in the jungle, black sap, cat loins, steam, gum-yellow tree root, brown sleeping sun. 'In the morning the head-hunter & me found we had got kinda attached to one another, so he gave me one of his shrunken heads, and I gave him my I.D. bracelet, which he'd been castin' eyes on all along.' 'And do you still have the shrunken head?' 'No, I gave it to a friend, 3-4 years ago. But now I wish I had it. Yes sir, I surely wish I did!'
I sit, sipping my coffee, which has grown thick & sappy in my mouth. This boy, now only 20, what will he be? 'Gary what will you be?' He smiles firmly.
'A surgeon.'

39
The hospital bus bumbled rickety away, carrying us to a short outing in the country. We sat quietly like easter eggs in a basket. The bus stopped in a clearing, orange with sun and wild poppy-seed smell. We got down, still wary, but talking together as we moved toward the river. In the river we saw what had leaked somehow out of our minds—its juice smelled acid like lime, or grasshopper blood. My heart beating stronger, I sat on a great rock with my face turned to the sun; and the others huddled around me. Marjorie, a tall woman with a scarred face who was getting ready to serve time for embezzling, rolled her jeans up to her thighs & walked right into the river juices. I approved of that. Flexing my naked feet, which felt small & cramped, I slipped a few toes into the water & stood up. In a long swooping arc I fell into the water, my feet slapping over the rock moss, & lay on my back staring into the sun. The water lapped my chin.
'Be careful!' someone cried. I got up, holding to the rock. 'I'm not hurt,' I said. What I always say when knocked down. A black bruise ran up under my dress as far as my waist, invisible until I later swabbed away the pebbles & murk. But that was not the nature of the hurt. I lie in bed, not thinking of lying in the river staring into the sun. Unripe. Praying for caution. Stilling the nervous voice of the stunned will.

40

Walking in the desert, I saw a lady in a blue cloak coming to me. She had bare arms and feet, a flowing embroidered dress, and a necklace of rubies and ebony around her throat. Her hair was bone white and fell to her ankles. When she came close to me, I saw that she was very old, but her mouth was still red and her eyes were black. I am a queen, and you, my daughter, are a princess. Give me your hand so that I may give you a sign of your powers.' I held out my hand. From the folds of her cloak she withdrew a dagger, and, grasping my wrist, stabbed my hand three times. Tears fell from my eyes as I shielded the hand in my dress. 'O, why did you do that?' I cried out. The lady opened her mouth and a silver snake came out. It wound itself around her neck and strangled her. In her final seizure I bent down and looked at her face. The skin fell away from it, and beneath was the face of a wolf. A single crystal drop lay at the base of its fangs. I knew that that was poison. I said aloud, 'Is it right for me to bury this strange creature?' A desert mouse heard me. 'Go away,' it said. 'That is a great witch, & it is left to a great wind to bury her.'

41

Marie always kept a perfumed lace handkerchief in her pocket. As she aged she tried to find new resources for it; it was her most significant possession. At my house she mopped my babies' noses with it, dabbed at her weepable eyes, and even tried to mop up carrot peelings & cucumber seeds with it. 'Marie,' I pleaded, 'you'll stain your handkerchief.' 'I treasure every stain on this handkerchief,' she whispered intensely. 'This was one of Munie's nosebleeds in 1937. This was port wine that a Norwegian diplomat spilled on the Regency Hotel tablecloth at the May Day dinner in 1944. This was Arthur's sputum when his first warning fit of coughing—' 'Oh, for God's sakes,' I said. 'You should hang it on the wall for a shrine.' Marie's face lit ecstatically. 'Oh yes! How lovely. How sweet! A shrine!' We moved her to an uncle's, where she sits in the garden crocheting, pasting, modeling, and gilding the thread, paper, glue, gold stars, twigs, tinsel, and clay she has purchased for her handkerchief's shrine. Sometimes I miss her and her musky, teary handkerchief, but I know that all her thoughts are with the dear Lord, and He can take care of her and her handkerchief better than I can.

42

After a separation of 7 days, we made love like a stampede of elephants. Then it was like a Florentine fountain at sunrise. And finally he came to me like the earth-colored bulls in Etruscan paintings, the ones with kingly, demon-blue cocks; and together we rode a long space, a long golden space, a long, liquid golden space, to the center of an ocean, an eye, an ocean's navel, where there were plumed birds with silver feet and burning orange eyes.

43

An old Sicilian lover of mine visited me in a dream. He was angry, and whenever he threw back his long black hair, wisps of it stood out like knives against the window light. 'I am dead, and you belong in the dead world with me.' 'No,' I said. He struck me once across my left hand. When I woke, the fingers lay on the pillow.

44

Merifa, 50 yrs. old, shock treatment burns on your arms, your hair is turning green. Your mind flew out of its canary cage a few months ago, perhaps it feels freer that way. She wails at me, 'Why are you sitting there?' wringing her nailbroken hands. 'Are you nervous? Aren't you going to get up now? Don't you need to go to the bathroom? It's so cold here. Why are your feet crossed that way? Are you nervous? I forget your name. Why are you sitting there? Are you cold? Are you nervous?' 'No, Merifa, are you?' 'I'm nervous. Yes. I'm nervous. I can't sleep any more. Are you nervous? Why are you just sitting there?' I said, 'Don't worry about that, Merifa, I'm just waiting for someone.' Turning away she shook her head, hair shivering. A cold hand over her mouth she whispered, 'Oh yes. She is. She's nervous.'

45

Speaking to Ramakrishna, I asked him why my bones are so small. 'Did they shrink in my illness?' He laughed. 'My bones are as small as yours,' he said. 'But you don't live in the world,' I said. He laughed again. 'Neither do you,' he said, shaking his monkey head. He gave me a picture of Mother Kali; but as I have to go back to the world, I put it away in a suitcase.

46

The field with its dormice and titmice belongs to the Mother of the Universe. Pink Spanish houses with arched windows & green tile roofs belong to her. Cypress forests, banyan forests, & a coconut tree forest are given to her. Cactus, glass and silk, honey, scrub palms, painted tile stairways, domed ceilings, dates, ivory, leather and sassafras are from her. I bitterly deny the right of men to house Her with acoustical tile and metal but when the Mother was told of me, she laughed with an ancient, agile, mummy's tongue. She cradles atrocities in her arms like infants. Those of her babies she drops, while dancing the tarantella, are trampled under her feet. Who knows why others are more tenderly held and suckled? She suckles praying mantises, but not emperors. No, but often she suckles garbage men, and—nearly always—the short order cooks of all-night diners. Her favorite signs are known to be the Sphinx & the single bit of golden earring in a gypsy's ear. And if you know of any Gypsies still alive, that is a thing you ought to let them know.

47

Anna eating, this is strange eating. Eating with nostrils arms feet, 15,831 spirals of rigatoni macaroni, and meringue smeared on your cheeks. Taking a black lacquered mirror from your pocket, you spit out your tongue to examine a mouthful of oatmeal. Tonight you will disembowel yourself with a nail file, examining your innards attentively with the lacquered mirror; but when you put them back, you'll see, they will not fit.

48

The black blades of a windmill turn. The father, cigarmouthed, a fishercap pulled over his eyes, leans on the plow, driving the ox round and round again. The mother, hair knotted, wristbones gleaming, smacks the laundry against the stones. Black blades of the windmill turn, man and his ox push, woman flails the linen shirts on the old white stones. A baby with its knees bare to the sun sits in the windmill door. In her hands a package of salt crackers. She munches the paper package cover, a slippery freshness in her mouth. Windmill, munch, oxsaunter, munch, laundryslap, munch. Sunlight on my knees, smoothness in my mouth. Suddenly the package cover bursts. The baby's mouth startles. Salt

manna bursting in her mouth! She chews baby lovefury, eyes glassy little fires, both fists pressed to her mouth. Holding a few crumbs in each hand, she wags them at the sun; kneejiggle, knees sprinkled with manna, toejiggle, salt between her toes. Manna! Salt soft manna. The black blades of the windmill turn, man and his ox push, and woman flails the linen shirts on the old white stones. Salty feet, salted lap, salt stones, salted sky.
Salt. Ox. Slap.
Windmill turning, poisoned sea, swordfish floating over the earth.
Baby knees, baby tears, baby weeping for salt.
For sun.
For salt.

49
The fish that eat me eat the moon, the fish that eat the moon eat grass eat glass. The eaten candles the eaten cathedrals. The eaten speech of animals I loved.

50
A lean Mexican poet with a broken nose went to the underworld to find a god with a perfect nose. He found him lying under an altar of purple quartz. 'Give me power to sing great poems,' said the poet, 'or I'll take your nose.' 'Sure,' said the god, feeling his nose reflectively. For 62 years the poet wrote like an immortal. On the day of his death he excused himself from his deathbed to return to the underworld. There he laid his collected works, bound in satin & gold leaf, at the feet of the sleeping god; removed his nose, & went home. He died an Aztec.

THREE POEMS FROM
IX ECLOGHE

ANDREA ZANZOTTO

Translated by Vittoria Bradshaw

FOR THE NEW WINDOW

There shines the window of the green a long
long time compounded, dream by dream,
orchard or meadows I ignore; but how much rime
before being convinced, how much snow.

Green of the corn lifting your head mocking
between the uncertain gold and the void:
you, my window, and you, sky, bringing
me amid quiet stars the blaring satellites

the human game has launched, with glares
of science fiction, to woo in light orbits
the hills and the beef on the ploughed field
not astir beholds them, and the vine and the moon.

Oh my window, unquenchable purity.
To make you I spent all I owned.
Now, not happy, in sheer poverty,
still all your gifts I do not savor.

But soon
you will give me all I yearned for.

II ECLOGUE: THE SILENT LIFE

to M.

I
We still sit together
among hills in the familiar forest.
Tender shoots from our temples we brush off,
suns and thistles and lively fields I brush
off you, friend. Oh grass ascending
towards dark everlasting, towards
qui omnia vincit.
And winds quench and renew
at every flux of hours and water
our souls.
But here we sit intent
always on a mute constant guard.
Tender will be my voice and humble
but not cheap,
radiant in the throat
—that shade should never touch—
radiant will be your nuptial,
Sunday voice.
We will not be powerful, not praised,
we will accrete hair and brows
to live
leaves, clouds, snows.

Others shall see and know: the power
of other skies, of bountiful
restoring
atmospheres, of any frantic paradox,
others shall move history
and fate. For us
the mothers in the kitchen watch
over poor fires, glean
soft wood in yards already girdled
by void. Scant milk
will feed us
foolish amiable useless
till old age removes us, which prepares
in the next field the ill-flowered
beds and the faltering
heart throbs, the pain
and the irreversible stasis.

II

But of my smile you will know
the steadfast imploring
through ages like a wound;
of yours I shall know the dawn at each dawn.
As light burgeon I shall know you:
to what extent you will open, to what extent oblige us with,
light events.
Harmless drugs, March storms;
orchards iridescent and wan, sinecures
for minds and hands soft with allergies;
readings by Summers' haze,
readings by rains, amid endless thorns of rains
At times Urania with the truth
will face us, split like an armored fruit:
supreme skies,
flights the solstitial
night rekindles,
gems of remotest
hatred and loves, toil
of glaring hydrogen:

here laid in the water of a planet
for profiles of crocuses and dragonflies.
Perhaps I shall raise to you my lashes
to you my mouth whereto the inert
waiting did temper speech, existence.
And even down the earth,
tomorrow my last token
will gleam clear with enthusiasm of stars,
with swift convulsed hopes.

We shall have distances upturned
mirrors which relinquished stolen images
flowers emerged from walls to adore you.
We will be a sole anxiety a sole oblivion.

III ECLOGUE: THE VINTAGE

I
Fall, now soon. And the colchicum
on meadows and the moon, as queen, forthcoming
and the bounteous fruit in the adyta of night
and the brooks gleaming centipedes.
Live things, ah, lives that now
I deem as lost. Who, tardy,
will linger to berhyme you?
But somewhere you await me, with some token
of humanhood, the most limpid, at the limit.
Soft side of the grass,
moon side in the day,
peace in retrieval, slow trees,
authority and substance.
Yes, it is a silly drunkenness
this one, it will not last. With the sweet
colchicum and sleep which beyond me gleams
like an expansive richest rose
I will also recover the supreme, the superfluous, the azure.

In it
I restore myself: so little
suffices the precarious soul
(refraction that now
falls sham, and I ignore the reason)
so little to return,
to be: ray
allayed with heavens where to fall.

II
Fall was the time
of the large yield,
vintage much longed for, when
you existed, poetry: pure
A motion, a mode, ultimate, of the azure
self-content and contenting
also the vanquished, the alienated.
You were, you were not: maimed
in this, more than guilty;
you moonlike beyond the forest ever,
ever with the vain ray
even in the forest shedding. But now
in other dusks you flow, source tainted
with barbarism, in other river beds, defect and perdition.
Interferences rise, hold fast
where your inarticulate
heart failed, your rhythm to which
the unfailing temple—it alone—closely listened.
Here. But I am immune
and guiltless: that much I dare say.
And I keep you for the azure
—only at times
(as for the Autumn, father, pallet, food)—
for the azure of hierophancy
which warrants every passion, every shapelessness strangles.
Exudation, smoke, light
of images, of encounters, of conatus
. . . .
. . . .
Password
of other millions of years, other extinct eons,
trivial slogan. We
. . . .

PETITES SCULPTURES

J-F. BORY

NOTE 1

The singular error of Kleist, of Novalis, and of Mallarmé led us to the idea of grasping total reality, the totality of experience, by an act of literature. Since then, everything has induced us to believe that with the end of writing there could be no more reason to write.

Moreover, caught up in this furious attempt to recapture total reality, writers no longer saw the necessity of sentences, of words.

What should be most important is the whole, and the whole is the book. The book insofar as sentence, the book insofar as writing in a temporal development, the book insofar as modulation are concerned.

Literary Labor. (15 x 20 x 12 centimeters)

Portrait of the Author on a Horse. (15 x 20 x 22 centimeters)

The book of the past analyzed a situation; the new book translates a state of being. Moreover, at present the aim of an author is achievement, to become this state of being. To write is to want to say everything, and to want to say everything is to want, in the final analysis, to speak no more.

At any rate, the end purpose of the book is that there be an end to books.

For it is no longer a matter of understanding or expressing but of being caught up in the very text and texture of the everyday world.

Each visual book is a key book, a method, somewhat like the first page of an inventory. Therefore, with new books the reader will begin to read his own text, his environment-text into which he will be permanently plunged. And so the endless reading begins.

Already today, the spirit balks at reading a traditional linear text; for it will be from now on a matter of reading the world-text. Soon, even the understanding of this book through the reading of its text will have become useless.

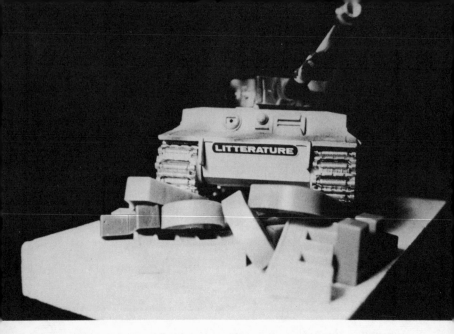

Literature.

Our books prepare for this great explosion. It is a matter of seeing here the disposition of an emotion located in our space . . . the book as method manifests, demonstrates, brings forth concrete forms.

By reading and waiting, doubt and concentration become living things between our hands. And so, since the book coexists with language, reading dispenses incalculable instants, fractions of time during which a concept surges, astounds, annihilates.

Ceaseless reading . . .

NOTE 2

It is likely that countless numbers of books besides ours will eddy and swirl in a void of libraries. Such books will be unlike ours. They will consist of pages and words that are fundamentally different. For example: characters or signs that are not apparently linked, that are never repeated but are nevertheless language. Writing that is perpetually evolving; not like ours over a period of centuries but in minutes.

Changing from page to page. Books in which the signs of language will consist of the spaces between the words. Books without pages, or even books without end. Books with thousands and thousands of pages that never stop at a cover. Books through which the light will move as slowly as words are pronounced. While here, the text begins its formation from the blank page. Books in which the page will form, will grow from signs. Books without breaks to separate the letters one from the other and books in which words will know more separation than in ours. Books in which words will be real and where each page will be a god. Fluid books that will branch out in time—one part of the book readable now—another in five centuries . . . Books of jungles or of vines or of roads. Books that are different according to every fundamental law.

We want to create a monster of a book that will heave up from this universe, giving birth to a monster of a book-universe, and it little matters if this universe must be destroyed.

Literature.

Rauchenberg in the Early Morning. (15 x 20 x 2 centimeters)

The book that explores space, that is at the same time always open and always closed.

Page after page. The books behind us are dead. The pages ahead are not yet born.

In order to arrive at the book, one must travel across pages that no sun will ever lighten, pages that open into nowhere, that are tortuous and full of infected words and grand but black and oily phrases that whirl on invisible axes . . . Nothing again can venture across the great pages of the shipbook except gigantic words without meaning that take up permanent lodging there . . . it is a terrible trip on the shipbook that gives its pilot-author nausea and nightmares . . . travel . . . the formless flaming, icy cemeteries of history . . . travel . . .

For beyond one finds the book!

THREE POEMS

Translated by Michael Roloff

WHAT I AM NOT, DON'T HAVE, DON'T WISH, WOULDN'T LIKE—AND WHAT I WOULD LIKE, WHAT I HAVE AND WHAT I AM.

(sentence biography)

What I am NOT:
I am no spoilsport
I am no mealymouth
I am no child of sadness.

What I am not FIRST, SECOND and THIRD OF ALL:
First of all I am no dreamer, second of all I am no recluse,
and third of all I am not an inhabitant of the ivory tower.

What *I* am not:
I am no voting bloc.

What I UNFORTUNATELY am not:
Unfortunately I am no hero
Unfortunately I am no millionaire.

129

What I am not THANK GOD:
Thank God I am no automat
Thank God I am not someone with whom you can do as you please.

What I FINALLY am not:
Finally I am nobody's fool
Finally I am no insane asylum attendant
Finally I am no garbage dump
Finally I am no charity organization
Finally I am no soul saver
Finally I am no credit union
Finally I am no doormat
Finally I am no information bureau.

What I ADMITTEDLY am not, BUT ALSO am not:
Admittedly I am no coward, but I am also no sadsack.
Admittedly I am no scorner of progress, but I am also no worshipper
    of everything new.
Admittedly I am not a militarist, but I am also not a proponent
    of a lazy peace.
Admittedly I am no supporter of violence, but I am also
    no scapegoat.
Admittedly I am no pessimist, but I am also
    no bright-eyed utopian.

What I am NEITHER NOR:
I am neither a nationalist nor do I believe in the abolishment
    of all distinctions
I am neither a fan of dictatorships nor a defender
    of a misunderstood democracy.

What I don't HAVE:
I have no desire to put my nose into other people's business.

What I don't WANT:
I don't want a fuss.

What I don't want, BUT:
I don't want to say that everything is fine, but—

What I DON'T want, BUT ALSO don't want:
I don't want to enumerate all my good qualities, but I also
    don't want to be guilty of false modesty.

What I WOULDN'T LIKE:
I wouldn't like to cast the first stone.

What I would LIKE:
I would like for us to get along.

What I WANT:
I only want the best for you.

What I have WANTED:
I have always wanted the best.

What I USED TO HAVE:
I used to have similar opinions earlier on.

What I HAVE:
I have problems of my own.

What I AM:
I am for it.

What I am BESIDES:
Besides, I am here too.

What I am ALSO SOMETIMES, BUT THEN AGAIN:
Sometimes I also feel that it can't go on like this, but
    then again—

What I AM:
It's *me*!

ABSTRACTION OF THE BALL
THAT FELL IN THE RIVER

As children we often sat at the edge of the river Sunday afternoons watching the soccer game from where we sat at the midfield line. Whenever the ball fell in the water near where we were sitting we ran alongside the river and with long poles fished the ball out of the water. We could take our time doing this since each time the ball fell in the water another ball that was kept in reserve was put into play from the sideline. We ran as fast as the ball was carried along by the river until we fished it out always just before it reached the wall of the weir. As a rule, the river flowed slowly enough so all we had to do was walk alongside the ball. But once when the river was swollen we had to run.

At the edge of a soccer field, which is situated by a river, a number of children are in the habit of having fun running alongside the ball whenever it falls into the river during the course of play; that is, they run alongside the ball from the midfield line to the end of the field and fish it out of the water only there. Once when the river was swollen, the children had to run very quickly.

Children walk alongside the ball each time it falls in the river at midfield. They fish the ball out of the water only at the end of the field. When the river is swollen the children run very quickly.

Persons walk from the midfield line of a soccer field to the end of the field alongside an object that is drifting in the river at the edge of the field. At the moment when they reach the end of the field the referee whistles half-time. When the river is swollen and the persons have to run they come to a stop alongside the object at the end of the field shortly before the half-time whistle blows.

Someone is walking along the edge of a soccer field next to an object that has fallen in the river. He gets under way 30 seconds before the last minute of the first half of the game. At the very moment he has reached the end of the field and stands next to the object the referee blows the half-time whistle. When the river is swollen he reaches the end of the field together with the object precisely one second before the whistle blows and after he has gotten under way simultaneously with the object 10 seconds before the referee blows his whistle.

In order to traverse half the length of a playing field (playing field length = 90 meters) someone requires 1 minute, 30 seconds. When he has to run he requires for the same distance only 9 seconds.

It takes someone 90 seconds to traverse 45 meters. Running it takes him 9 seconds.

90 sec————45 m
1 sec————speed x m

9 sec————45 m
1 sec————speed y m

$$90\,x = 45$$
$$9\,y = 45$$
$$x = \frac{45}{90}$$
$$y = \frac{45}{9}$$
$$x = \frac{1}{2}$$
$$y = 5$$

As children we walked on Sunday afternoons at a speed of one half meter per second alongside the soccer ball when it was kicked from the playing field into the river. But when the river was swollen we had to run alongside the ball at a speed of five meters per second to fish the ball out of the water before it would be washed over the wall of the weir.

THE INNER WORLD
OF THE OUTER WORLD
OF THE INNER WORLD

"WE:"

Only when they take the one who's been shot away
do we recognize
by the big round nail heads
on the soles of the boots of the one who's been shot
that he was innocent

We are in Nashville, Tennessee:
but when we enter the hotel room
and have looked at the issue of PLAYBOY
with the partially visible, glinting, inside
of Ursula Andress' nose
what begins to seize us
—in lieu of perplexity over the fact
that we are in Nashville—
is the inside of Ursula Andress' nose

We go to Prague:
there it is around nine in the evening
we read about the time of quiet in the streets
but when we step on the street at nine
it is high time
for a last-ditch effort
to stay clear of company

We find ourselves in a department store:
we want to use the escalator
to get to the toy department
where we want to purchase building blocks
but since the escalator has temporarily stopped
the immobile escalator
on which we are walking up
transforms itself into our breath
which we are holding

and the held breath
which we now exhale
because the escalator is suddenly moving again
implodes into a pile of building blocks—

We go inside ourselves:
there
when we are furious
it is late afternoon as in a factual report about an assassination:
when we become tired
all the keys dangling on their appointed hooks on the hotel
        key board let
our eyes fall shut:
at the same time as the moon
appeasement rises there:
astonishment transforms itself into a white sheet
covering the sweets in a candy store after closing time:
and together with the feeling of shame we are overcome by
        the acrobat in
the circus who, after his number with the beaming smile
        has failed,
spreads his arms wide—

Once when we are without a care in the world
we see a cross-country runner in a blue gym suit
running past us
but then we see
that the cross-country runner is running down a street:
because we are no longer without a care in the world;
and finally we see
that the cross-country runner is not running down the street in
        a gym suit
but in a long coat
that interferes with his running:
because we are uneasy;
and then see
while leaning out the train window
how the cross-country runner is waving to us:
as a sign
that we're again without a care in the world—

Feeling awkward transforms itself into a green traffic signal
toward which we are walking
while it is still green
and the yellow signal
toward which we rush
switches over to the display window of the grocery store
during a holiday
and in the empty grocery store the sausage slicing machine
    transforms itself
into a fully loaded elevator in which we ride with lowered eyes
    when we
feel awkward—:

So let us agree to call innocence
shoe nails
perplexity
hotel room
inescapability
nine o'clock
indecisiveness
a stationary elevator
self-consciousness
a crowded elevator
and patience
the usherette in a movie house
waiting in the dark near the screen
with a case in her hands
until the young girl who is on-screen
has offered the merchandise
which the elderly usherette
quite self-consciously
when the house lights come on
as though she was in a crowded elevator
will now offer to us
or vice versa
or vice versa—

We enter our consciousness:
as in a fairy tale it is early morning there
on a meadow in early summer:

when we are curious;
as in a Western it is noon there
with a large calm hand placed on the bar:
when we are tense;
as in a factual report about a sex crime
it is early afternoon there
on a muggy late summer day
in a barn:
when we are impatient;
as in a radio news report
foreign troops are crossing the border toward evening:
when we are confused;
and as in the dead of night
when there is a curfew
the stillness of the streets begins to spread
when we can't express ourselves before anyone—

Someone sees so many objects
he becomes indifferent to them—
someone sees so many indifferent objects
he gradually loses himself out of his consciousness—
then he sees an object
which he does *not* want to see
or which he would like to see *more* of
or which he would like to *have*
so that the object becomes an object
with which he would like to pander to the desire of his eyes
an object
of his will
of his ill-will
and he *regards* it
or *rejects* it
or wants to *have* it
and he becomes conscious—

Only when the defendant is sentenced
do we recognize
that the defendant was accused.

NINE POEMS FROM
THE EVERYDAY BOOK

CARL RAKOSI

To George Oppen

THE POET

When he sat down to his desk
                              in the morning
there was a voice
                    weeping
from the personal
                    which could not bear its frailty
and longed for alleviation
in some lovely figure or perception.

Sometimes it spoke
                    as if it knew it was going to be published:
"I will never sacrifice man for art."

It needed no one
and was neither modest nor superior,
just sure and straight.
When he heard it, he knew he had a good thing
and wrote it down,
at first plain
            and then as high character,
as if he were discovering his nature.

But the commitment had already been made
to honesty and clarity.
Why then did he have to go through
                              all that strangeness?

THE MOMENT

The simile flew
            out of chance
to the poet
            belly aglow
but when he looked in
                  for his breath
the light expired
            as from a firefly.
Yet on the reader's earth
this was a pyramid of Cheops.

                        O eternal
is its element!

THE EXECUTION

poet opens a box:
                    empty!
Where is the god?
                    in syntax . . .
on linguistic wires . . .
                    out of sight!

And longing?
                    where's the god of that?
It has been Englished.
                    It bleeds no more.

FRAGMENT

The big birds
                    look impervious.
The young child's image
of his father
                    with imperishable head
goes down with him to the grave
and all the great unmoved ones
                    look long distances
but inside are small
for sweetness from the knowledge of mortality
                    spurts
as from a spring
                    and only when it runs dry
needs the bird
                    austere, immovable
seeing beauty in it.

Only language is both sweet and enduring.

THE HISTORY OF MAN

That cry of agony
                    from a carious tooth:
the man from the age
                    of orogenies
has left his parameters
                    in us
and a memory of his ordeal.

TUNE

Today I was pleased by the image
                    of the Japanese wrestler
legs apart
            hair tied in the back
looking like Turkey
                    astride the Anatolian fault

and a voice in me
                    cried
"Let us go down to the river
                    and find Armenia

and listen again to that way of speaking in Vasari:
'It is related that Giorgione
                    in conversation
with certain sculptors
                    at the time
when Andrea del Verrocchio was engaged with his bronze horse . . .' "

HOW TO BE WITH A ROCK

The explicit ends here.
                    Outer is inner.
It is all manifest.
                    Its character is durity.
There lies its charisma.

By nature it is Pangaea.
                    It has its own face
and its own tomb,
                    the way it stands
unmoved by destiny,
                    a model for the mind.
We can only be spectators.
                    All is day within.

"Go to the village,"
                    I tell my wife,
"and bring back a chicken,
                    an onion, a goose
and an apple
            and we'll lie here
and repopulate this Siberia."

It is in Genesis.
A strange god,
            all torso
and without invention or audacity.

It can be accused of both plutonism
and the obvious.
                    The closest human thing to it
is the novocained tooth
                    its Medusa hair now fossilized.

It can be bequeathed to one's heirs
with the assurance that it will not depreciate
or be found irrelevant.

AIE!

there's the greenwood fern
and the open woods
and the smell of hay
and the eye of a frog
and a fern signature
left in a coal

and there is fern by analogy,
a most ancient weed.

RIDDLE

In the dead of night
the caribou slept.

The possibility of not knowing
what you are
had not yet been conceived.

It is the original forest.
There is peace.

The wolf has eaten.
He goes into a long howl
to give his location.

If the hunter does not find him,
he'll live seven years.

A box is a box.
Integrity has been defined.

SHOOT!

JAMES PURDY

Boogee Boome was an older girl who had a mud-fence for a face, and lived and worked in a big plastic hospital. One prolonged June evening, inspired by the national hot-cakes seller *How to Be In, Expensive, and Publish Bi-Weekly,* by Professor Jessie Rolled Oats, Boogee phoned Hollywood, U. S. A., on her princess portable, though her hospital insurance didn't begin to cover even local calls. The great celluloid mogul Attar Wimminsure happened to pick up the wire. As a matter of fact, Attar was at that identical moment scrap-diving for a script about a girl with a mud-fence for a face, and when Boogee laid her maidenhood ambition on the line in terms of money-angle-film-book, he saw on the acrylic wall eight figures going into nine. Keeping Boogee mooning on one wire, he private-dialed Robinson Useto, a big downtown editor who was getting ready to go uptown, on another.

"Robinson Useto, I've got the biggest plastic pile of 'in' on my hands since the days of vampires. Girl with a mud-fence for a face!"

"Mud, eh?" Robinson considered. "Sounds way-out expensive for us little downtown people here."

"Not soapsuds expensive, Robbie . . . But I'll level with you because you're pure prestige . . . Boogee can't even write a run-on sentence yet, let alone spread her plot into a full-length book."

"Aha, Wimminsure. So we're to be put to hard labor writing her little novel for your great big movie."

"Freeze us if you will, Robinsin: it's your New York prerogative
. . . But now hear good, for this is the big *it*, though you stuck-up
downtown people make me puff. While you were sniffing, I keyed
in Lit-Gilt-Doubledip on my computer wristband, and what comes
back as their reply? Our film will be one of their electric-circus
book selections, with the revolving rose lights display in all their
windows from here to Peking—same deal they give me for my
smash *Kitty Was a Mink*. Further, and bite on this, 'twill win the
national hot-cakes award before we get her naked on the jacket."

"As a gentleman, Attar, I can't fight you," Useto's voice came
fairly steady. "Sign us up for mud in Onion Square!" he finished,
and motioned for his assistant to put more ice bags on his stomach.

And so in less time than it takes a New York critic to review a
book (nine minutes, twenty seconds), and while the money fell
like slush, Americans all over everywhere, as only a free people
can, were standing *in*, or rather, as those supersensitive sugar-
mouthed snooties Button Nitwood of *Esquirm* and Guff Whuff of
Newsqueak would say, standing *on* line in front of the 400,000
Doubledip windows, waiting of course for the arrival of the film.
And though the great daily pundits Boore and Pepscout had gone
off to the state preserves for a long-deserved blackout, the morning
the movie arrived in hardcovers, Ellis Smother-Wheelcox (wonder-
ful, magnanimous, ubiquitous Wiltroot Cheep had not yet made
his big play as a straightman from Oxford), Ellis Smother-Wheelcox,
I say, told his family-newspaper audience that he, for one reviewer,
had cried like two babies after sitting down to finish the story of
Mud-Fence's finding love too late for marriage in a hospital, but
cashing in just the same on her first clean million. And the world's
bulkiest book section spread Boogee's entire biog from bandages
to bandwagon in an immortality profile-spread.

As Boogee said while on tour with Mogul Wimminsure: "It's not
so much what you can *do* for money in this grand old U. S. A.—
you can't do a loving thing without it!"

DRY RADIANCE

Selected Poems

ALEKSIS RANNIT

Translated by Henry Lyman

Translator's Introduction: Listening to Aleksis Rannit speak his poems, one is impressed by the meditative resonance of his native tongue, Estonian. Together with Finnish and Hungarian, it belongs to the Finno-Ugric language group. Unlike familiar Indo-European languages, it is characterized by having no sibilants other than a soft "s" and by a predominance of vowels. (There are six vowels to every four consonants, and some words are composed of vowels alone: õu—yard, courtyard; öö—night.) Estonian has both long and short syllables, as in the classical languages, and an extralong syllable as well. It also has almost complete syntactic flexibility. (A sentence of seventeen words can be composed in an equal number of ways, partly because of the existence of fifteen grammatical cases.) And, like all Western tongues except English, Estonian makes active use of the familiar personal pronoun thou—sina. In these respects, it is one of the more intimate, supple, and melodious of languages, very suitable to poetry and song.

Although the earliest discovered printed Estonian verse dates from the 1600's, it was only at the turn of the last century that Estonian literary poetry began to flourish. Until then, the most usual form of verse was the folk song, of which at least 400,000 examples

146

have been produced by this Baltic country with a population of only one million. The older Estonian songs, such as the 10th–13th-century heroic ballads that comprise the folk epic "The Son of Kalev" (Kalevipoeg), *were phonetically quantitative (their cadence dependent upon the merging of syllabic length with metrical accent), whereas in literary poetry this natural metrical system was for the most part ignored. The postsymbolist poet Villem Ridala (1885–1942) reinstated the quantitative method to some extent, but Aleksis Rannit, together with Estonia's foremost translators of classical poetry, Ants Oras and August Annist, brought about its full revival.*

As poet and critic, Rannit has divided his life between literature and the fine arts. Born in 1914 in Kallaste, Estonia, he studied art history and Russian literature at the universities of Tartu and Vilnius, and aesthetics and classical archaeology at the University of Freiburg. He was a founder of the International Association of Art Critics and a professor of art history at Freiburg, as well as guest lecturer at other European universities. Later, as a director of French Cultural Affairs in postwar Germany, he organized large exhibitions of leading French artists, many of whom he had previously met in France. In 1953, Rannit came to the United States, and for the past eleven years he has been Curator of Russian and East European Studies at Yale. His essays on poetry, art, and comparative aesthetics have been published both here and abroad, and in 1964 he was elected a full member of the International Academy of Arts and Letters.

Much of Rannit's poetry has been translated into German, Russian, Lithuanian, and Hungarian, yet it is barely known in English-speaking countries. (Indeed, this is unfortunately true for all Estonian writers, of whom there are some of real international stature.) A small number of his poems have been translated into English by Ants Oras, Emery E. George, Ruth Speirs, and Asta Willmann, while a limited collector's edition of my own renderings was published by Adolf Hürlimann (Zürich, 1970).

The poems translated here include: several written to Rannit's friend Eduard Wiiralt, the noted Estonian etcher-engraver who lived most of his adult life in Paris and died there in 1954; "Signets," in which Rannit speaks as though through the voices of particular artists, musicians, and poets, ancient and modern; and "Form and Freedom," a grouping of miscellaneous items together with a selection from a group of sea-and-island compositions ("Via purgativa") begun while the author was traveling in Greece on a Ford Foundation grant. Needless to say, most of the rhythms and musical qualities of Estonian are inimitable in a language so remote as English. I have tried, nonetheless, to use comparable devices wherever possible, particularly with respect to certain kinds of euphony, and I believe that the translations are faithful to the atmosphere of the original poems.

Rannit's poetry acknowledges both some Western and Eastern European influences, symbolist and classicist predominantly, the strongest of which is the work of Paul Valéry. Beginning with a decorative lyric style, it eventually arrived at a union of classical form with classical and romantic content, symbolically reflected in the titles of the books themselves: Akna raamistuses ("Framed by the Window"), 1937; Käesurve ("A Grip of the Hand"), 1945; Suletud avarust ("Enclosed Distance"), 1956; Kuiv hiilgus ("Dry Radiance"), 1963; Kaljud ("Rocks"), 1969; Sõrmus ("The Ring"), 1972—names that refer variously to space, light, or strength, either bound in rigid form or suffused by some static quality. In fact, the very concept of enclosed or stilled energy presents itself repeatedly in the verse, in such oxymorons as "frozen infernos," "wave of rock," and "icy pulse." This apparent antithesis, an essential element of Rannit's poetics, may be termed, if you will, impassioned form.

His love of classical precision has been compared to that of the Parnassians or the Acmeists. Ants Oras, however, has rightly insisted that the verse is "sculptured and vibrant at one and the same time," while Rannit himself has described poetry generally as not only "the mathematically sensitive usage of language," but also "sacred geometry." Indeed, his work is characterized by both strict rhythm and intricately fluid harmonic arrangement. He uses, for the most part, classical metrical schemes—the elegiac distichs, for example, as well as trochaic, anapestic, and amphibrachic measures—but a type of free verse, too, that owing to its strong rhythmical coherence might itself be considered a metrical form. His meter is phonetically enforced by the quantitative technique, which places long vowels and consonants on the stressed part of each foot (the stress, in Estonian, always falling on the first syllable). In addition, there are many pauses, silent spaces within the poems, which, like rests in music, are a functional part of the rhythm. With respect to *harmony, the lines are frequently imbued with what the specialist in Eastern and Western European poetics Victor Terras has called "sound symbolism" and synchronized with inner and alliterative rhymes, very systematic in their usage.*

The poems are formalist not only in their mineral-like integrity, but also in their frequent statement of Form as an artistic and metaphysical ideal: the premise "Beauty / is / ugliness / cast into purity of form" provides Form with aesthetic, if not moral, omnipotence, and "I have broken faith with colour. / Now my verses measure for the line" advocates an ascetic reduction of phenomena to a form within, to their simplest inner design.

It is not surprising, then, that Cocteau called Rannit "l'artiste d'une solitude, d'une noblesse," or that Terras has described his aristocratic and art-conscious work as "studies in poetic form," as "a running Ars Poetica, *focused in the recurrent conceit of a victory of line over color," and Form over mere sentiment.*

Passion, too—symbolized variously by fire, waves, thunder, wind, the color blue—is constant in Rannit's poetry. It ranges from amores *("Venetian Venus," "Aliiki," "Medici Blue") to a more general sense of mystery and tenderness toward Being ("The Sea," "Cognition"). And although sentimentality is opposed ("Paul Cézanne"), pure creative energy is embraced, sometimes even to the detriment of order ("In the Fifth Power of Sleep"). On the whole, however, such an open acceptance is not allowed to extend to pantheistic extremes. In the same way that the intoning voice is conducted through an inalterable rhythmic structure and its emotion held, suspended within that mathematical frame, passion is always subject to the idea of Form, always kept within the bounds of substance: the winter sun is a stone; caresses are of hail; the rain is like sudden glass—generative, dynamic power is sealed in matter. In a metaphor such as "the wintry flame of form," symbols of each element are permanently fused: fire (emotionalism, the sensual, the Dionysian) merges with ice (asceticism, the spiritual, the Apollonian), and both are made identical to Form. What the poet strives to achieve, then, is the synthesis of these opposing forces. In many poems they do, in effect, become indistinguishable.*

Finally, Rannit's contemplation of this alliance proves religious. Where Valéry, his mentor, remains skeptical, opposing chaos with a categorical affirmation of the divinity of art, Rannit conceives of art as a journey through an illusory chaos toward an Existence that is confirmed by his own nostalgia for the unio mystica. *His poems are often psalms, hymns sung in quest and celebration of an unseen but recognized cohesive presence. They are meant to reflect the continuity of movement, "the soul of form," with which a divine creative reason imbues the world. Rannit defines poetry, accordingly, as an inviolable "dance of syllables, . . . the consensually pulsating expression of our spirit, . . . a kind of sorcery in which metaphorical thinking blends with authentic reality to create a mythical order." From that point of view, his own poetry may be regarded as ceremonial music, in which he seeks to voice, and thus to hear, an otherwise inaudible rhythm.*

Verses to Wiiralt

HE TOILS THE HOURS

He toils the hours, time his intimate,
his soul a secret script, and knows:
patience is the sister of mystery,
tirelessness the best of roads.

He — his own apprentice:
alchemist, printer, surgeon.
And the thickest shadow glistens.
And the slightest wrinkle turns profound.

He — this fencer of electric fire,
torero who can never miss the kill —
no jockey or juggler or mime,
but soldier of spirit and steel.

Line — flaxen fiber, arrow, shaft —
gentle as a girl's incurving arm.
Line — a shimmering oar across the lake,
the whitened sand on the dimming bar.

Line — a whipstroke, the tenderest caress,
skies of lazuli and the savage windstorm.
Line — hideous outcry, cloistral silence —
smiles of angels, the satanic frown.

And above it all, the master's hand,
as though it brushed aside the time,
out of the wintry flame of form, beyond
all thought and feeling, draws the line.

LINE

Love toward line,
toward thee, all illuminating power.
Thou all ennobling rune —
line of the thunderbolt and not the thunder.

All binding and all bounding line,
accurate as the rhyme of death:
Phidias, Ingres, Wiiralt,
Bach and Valéry.

I have broken faith with colour.
Now my verses measure for the line —
for thee, line perfection engendered
in the ascetic square of the mind.

SO I SEE THEE STILL

Near. Strange. Striding the Rue Royale.
So I see thee still. Ever. Towering.
Smiles of Leonardo, inquisitive, curl
in the flickering turns of thy mouth.

And for what words? Of thee
and all thy toil, mere syllables —
veils — but passionate esteem
for Méryon, or Robert Nanteuil.*

As though grazing lettered speech
whispered at the verges of thy lips,
thy voice turned in and spoke to *thee* —
and its flame was buried in thy mist.

And now thy gaze has dropped again.
But thy springing step is free, reinless —
the bustling mobs about thee, at thy hand
the stone of the December sun — and Paris.

Behind, the columns of the Madeleine
recede with grave and vivid pace —
Cannot Estonian mystique sustain
the cinders of Hellenic sacrifice?

Thou art silent, and in silence hast said
that a craftsman must deny and withdraw.
That craft be strictness of measure.
And temper. And compass. And law.

* Two noted French engravers.

A VIEW OF THE ATLAS MOUNTAINS

Clouds as light as olive wreaths,
lighter than mist or air or wind,
the silver edges of their leaves
thicker still than gentlest wine.

Atlas sleeps. The mammoth sleeps,
and in his lee the morning stirs
the supple dark. Pounding feet
dash the waking earth with fire.

These mythic groves
do not adorn a scene.
Their substance proves
the truth which gleamed

when love was still affection.
Their light grows deep. O Montparnasse —
the mirrors of thy streets grow dim.
My footfalls meet them, and cannot pass.

This air — as mute and clean
as untouched copper. This air.
The storm of desert suns.
The scent of streaming rays.

WIIRALT SKETCHING. CHARTRES, 1951

My deadened eye, thy quickening hand.
My buffalo eye, thy swordlike hand.

Blue as a sword, this yuletide Chartres,
thy senses touched by lithe, blue Chartres.

Blue as a sword, our distance rife with frost,
our double solitude and its thickening frost.

Riven from this icy stone, our time,
living in the fury of Bach's flame, our time.

In fiery extinction stilled, this eye, this hand,
my dimming eye, and fast against the fire, thy hand.

CANTUS FIRMUS

Carve
     into the Tree of Mind
song,
        line which cannot run.
Sink thy passion's
               fitful wind
in the still salt of reflection.

Signets

PAINTER

I cherish rusted colour
more than coloured gold.
Fine, dry contours
make things mild.

I veil even the dry, twilit wine
of blood in this arid mind —
my brushstrokes radiantly dry,
dry as dust the dimming line.

Oh but never ask me why
birds
     never sing
           at sea.

DIOSKORIDES* — TO BYRON
Stay,
    poet of thunder,
hear from my silence
             and know:

dearer to me than lightning

are the syllables'
          gradual
              flames.

  * Greek epigrammatist, third century B.C.

MARIE LAURENCIN

The elliptical eyes
and the still,
radiant flesh,
breathlike gestures
and a brush to dream —

to dance
the slow,
clear dance,
calm
on the blue canvas.

Even,
her dancing through
frozen infernos —

Marie Laurencin.

GIORGIO MORANDI

Furious thoughts enchained
let colour beat more pure.
So from Giorgio Morandi came
a simple splendour,
born
of song from canvas blind,
the luminous smell of line,
the glowing space of time
and the permanent ice of silence.

PAUL CEZANNE

Timeless painting need not weep,
or cradle sweet
                    delirium.
It measures the light
                    and shade of the true,
plumbing the space of Doric stone.

It is the crisp azure of cubes,
timelessly burnished through time —
and the wrinkled tablecloth, the furrows,
where none but I can see
        mountain ridges,
                        burnished snows.

SEXTUS PROPERTIUS

Cynthia's yellow gown.
My sullen, yellow
ochre heart.
Roma — Amor.

The carven
shadows of the moon,
languishing, overgrown
in the rugged, stone-
grey crystal of the dawn.

Under the dim
Italian pines
she walks beside me
in a chuckling gait,
whilst her fingers
whisper
soft, impudent
ruinous words
into the hollow
of my hand.

And suddenly — immense
raindrops dash,
like fanfares of glass.

DOCTRINE OF THE DELIAN STYLITE

Thou vast, mounting,
shoreless fire —
pour thyself slender
as the tapering spire.

Strike true as the Word,
precise as Memnon's sword.
Seek words, wordless —
measuring the heart.

MAGISTER PEROTINUS MAGNUS*

Let the verge of colour harden,
and never alter thy theme.
Know: a setting suits a diamond
colourless, radiant and serene.

Whatever blazes lit the night,
whatever embers linger in thy dawn,
trust unto the single light,
thy cold, unshaded light alone:
lightning which has crossed the diamond.

* First great French composer, who lived in the 13th century; called
in French "Pérotin le Grand."

JAAN OKS*

Net-houses, saunas, barns
let rain slip through
into constructions
of silence withdrawn.

Relapsed. But the recent cry
still passes to the soul.
And silence?

                In music
              silence
                  is the core.

* Estonian expressionist poet who died in 1918.

PABLO CASALS

Singing flame — instinctive style —
unshakable line of tone and flesh:

I drew thee, setting song in flight —
summoning a full, throbbing measure.

The violins grew still — and the flutes
alone ran on, foreseeing the sudden swing.

The indolent viola lied
                                thinly as a thrush —
and there lived
            only the sad, strict
                        flight of the cello's wing.

STEFAN GEORGE

Too low, our gusts of passion,
to kindle even ten bright psalms.

The five or six I chiseled glisten,
spear the oak tree, hover in the palm,

revel in my vineyard as if the agony were done —
and curdle all my thought with haughty rapture.

And clawed from the muted depths of stones,
drawn from the pith of wingéd flowers,

my verses roam the page's ashen snows,
and my dreaming surges into proud hosannas.

Form and Freedom

SMALL BEGINNING

The name of time
      is
             namelessness,
rivers,
     eyeless,
           forlorn.
Beauty
     is
       ugliness,
cast into purity of form.

TRINAKRIA°

Electron. Electrons.
Southeast wind —
mirror, dagger, gem.
In the piercing tenor
of an electric saw —
screams the sea gull.

Gulls — handkerchiefs departing —
flutter down without echoes
toward the meadows of the sea.

The Trinákrian night turns to stone,
and in thine eyes alone, Circe,
there hovers —
quivering with rage —
the glistening shred of the sky.

° Landscape in the *Odyssey*.

MOONLIGHT FRIENDSHIP

Thy subtle breast is not 'divine,' and yet
within it lives the tremoring of dusty bays,
sadness which has dreamed and never slept,
moonlight wandering the arches of Beauvais.

Our friendship, and the moon of 'yesterday'
have set so high on the horizon,
with the soundless warmth of thy breast
and its tenderly bloodless might.

Thou of the softly vibrant canvas
where Corot swept his brush —
the ethereal reed of thy waist
cries for that very dust.

Whosoever long has read Bonnard
or heeds Vermeer's unruffled step
would see the islands I desire —
the pain-purged islands I desire —
barely touched by thy cold and gentle breath.

LENDONAKIA

So faithfully recalled,
        Lendonakía,
unforgettable headland
        never visited by me.

Oblong trunks of mountains undersea.
Shavings of moonlight
        wavering in river pools.
Lanterns running the footbridge
        arching over the Káranis.

Dead windows of the bungalows.
Dead leaves, ringing in the heat.
Tree stumps and their deadened eyes.

The bastard of my shadow, multifaced.

    Lendonakía —
blister on the memory.

MEDICI BLUE*

Given but one colour to choose,
I choose the blue, to keep our union
and our words alive. Good — the paint still runs,
colour floating on the palette ebbs and flows.

For distances and depths the measure,
colour marks thy spirit and thy ken —
like the lucid ice of thy recent passion,
like the bluest shade of sound thou hast spoken.

Mistaken, he who can sense
but the breadth of cold in the blue tone —
for thou art the warmth of blue, the substance,
glowing from light that flows from within.

   * The official name of a certain warm-blue colour.

SKYRITIS*

Even from here —
the Skyrítian heights —
I see the waves.

Waves like tumblers hurled by friends.
Waves, steaming like livid steeds.
Waves like banners of the fallen.

* Mountain range in Greece.

VENETIAN VENUS

And rusted light on solitary sails,
and olive dusk in the air —
and under frayed threads trembling, frail,
glistening strands of thy hair.

And cruel, keen yearning breaking forth,
and a gentle hail of caresses —
and through my settling fingers pour
the golden waters of thy flesh.

LOVE

Drinking from light the wine
at the foot of the favorable palm —
from light the lucid wine —
two mouths, a single breath,
one of what is nothing.

And the wings of the palm tree sever
in the black mirror of joy.

TWO DISTANCES

So have I drunken, for days on end,
radiance absolute and pure
from the graven line of thy hand
and the stunning pride of thy colour.

Two distances, side by side,
fused in an elemental rhyme —
and I know not which was ice
or which becomes the flame.

Flame, our final refuge
from overclouded skies,
flings its hands into yearning
and keeps us madly and wise.

AT THE FORD OF THE RIVER

In the watery light of dawn,
    I see her washing the linen
        on the riverbank at the ford.

So, for the last farewell, she comes
    from the veined Ionian rocks,
        through the scattering gloom.

I turn, still gazing back,
and see her now, forever — struck
into the sheerest white
        of no sound.

O Light, what be thy name
when stiffened into crusts
of rime on the kithára's chords?

Olive trees, grey as the Ithacan winter,
    and hope consumed:
        so shall my mother be.

THE SEA

I come to thee, my sister, in the final hour of the sun,
I come again to thy waters, I bring thee my brittle bones —

and I, like a fish on dry land, savagely mouthing the air,
taste only thee, my single perception, single impulse and aim.

In the whitening silence, the ring of thy spiralling waves,
filling my breadth and measure, draws me into thy space,

grips me in the coil of thy forces — and instantly takes me hence.
. . . This is my journey from the death of life, this my ascent —

ascension into thy tenderest depths, O sinuous nocturnal sea,
and skyward over thy face — high in a glittering leap.

Bursting out above thee — the yellow globe of the moon unfolds,
slowly flowering the night, the leaden gold of his robes

silently rippling thy breast. And under the thrall of the moon,
pure and whole and true as the night, the rising dome of
        thy music.

But where begins thine ever shapen, ceaseless tidal run,
Whose strictly shaded stream instills harmonious continuum?

Every thread of current, every swift, capricious whirl,
passing to the cosmos, rules the symmetry of worlds.

Whispering sand, ebbing wind, drifting quills of gulls —
therein I hear thee issuing the planet's icy pulse —

and I sense: before the Myth, before the mutiny of dreams,
even before the Word — was Rhythm, and was Rhythm's claim.

Rhythm's light runs through thee, hews thy wave-borne realm
darker than the diorite, hard and fluent as the hardest stone

is supple and severe. Image of order, the ultimate ideal:
to be the very birth of crystal — the beginning of the
      upward curl;

to be the carven, upswept wave — forever winging,
      forever wrought;
to be the everlasting surge, imprisoned in this night of rock.

Can I, O Rhythm, with my doubting tongue, ever take thee for
      my own:
thou — Rhythm — O destiny unending — Rhythm — O still and
      perfect flow?

ALIIKI/ELEGIAC DISTICH

Desiring again — Aliiki — thy madly delicate touch,
tracing thy slumbering lips, guarding thy braid in my palm,
heeding, I cherish the hope that anew there burst into flower
thy breast's diminishing flame, and the icy silk of thy kisses.

Measure, Apollo, this measureless passion — our purest of loves.
Let the weariless hours be still, cast us anew into one:
the tormented roses of Tyre, wind-borne oceans of clouds,
the undulant cinders of evening, Medusa of the setting sun.

COGNITION

Rapt was I in the rows of waves
quivering in the wild sun,
and then — the sudden blows
of livid thunder.

Like a fist
the storm
fell upon the sea. A moment —
and bitterly morose
was the image of my joy.

And the shattered faces of the waves,
like powdered sugar once, once like emeralds,
bound me in a spell, and the cadence
of the old accord emitted lies.

So disarranged, the long beloved line
between the water and the sky —
and of the quickened metals of the sea
I might have created visions.

But the journey of the sentiment
fits more the journey of the mind,
the impassive tenderness of the sea —
the sea whose water gives us light —
and the blueness of a whetted knife:
the ultimate colour of peace,
the blue of ultimate purity
coveted by my song.

— So good-bye to the raging pen
and the mad flickering of storms:
I want pain enclosed in rhythm —
fire that tapers into form!

IN THE FIFTH POWER OF SLEEP

In the cube of logos,
in the fifth power of sleep,
beyond, bend far adrift
across thy deepmost calm,
where tall, mounting,
brittle masts of thought
can nevermore withstand
the flow of earthly music.

Fell them, and go down
upon the broad and splendid sea.
Sweep onward, singing words
the full spring swells cast high.
Then let the surge engulf thee
and the flames of the descending waves
caress thee into stillness free.

CYPRUS

Again this winter in the skies,
this cunning artist bowman,
the Cyprian rocks;
these russet crystals blaze
that content
        is only

        a fraction of form.

TROVIA°

Run for the Trovian shores,
                now the seas are risen,
now the ancient quiver
                breaks from the icy mist,

summoning the cry of spring —
                whose urgent rustling moan
sweeps upward black and wingéd,
                scattering the gravelled coast.

Heavier in thy nostrils now,
                the ring of the suspended sea —
the sheer, cascading isle,
                the scarp of stone, upheaves,

shivering as though thy fist
                had struck the sinews of a lyre —
and 'run for the Trovian shores'
                is now both a plea and a dare.

This hissing croft of water,
                grey and breathlessly aslant,
rises, curling at the crest,
                and yelling — thundering — descends.

The glittering blow of the wave,
                pitiless, hurls thee on —
riven from all thou wast —
                and the impulse of thy pain

lifts thee, strong and alien,
                like a drifting oar,
like a grave and fated word,
                toward the tottering morn.

° My Avalon.—A. R.

From what unbidden throat
                that bleak and withered cry?
Was it the sobbing of a gull,
                or a bittern blown astray?

And 'run for the Trovian shores'
                ever bewitches the mind,
singing thee further in
                on the booming arm of the tide.

Above, the cindered clouds,
                fluttering like monstrous crows.
Below, thy hair uncoils, bronze
                in the sullen, ashen glow

of the ever-nearing rocks —
                the keen-edged, dripping reef.
And a sudden rush of wind
                flings thee hither — spinning free —

like a slingstone, low and flat —
                choking on thy doubled pride —
thy face gone white with joy —
                as though the day were thine —

until that rearing wall of iron
                shuts forever on thy gaze —
and thy misfit body shatters —
                the splintered members drift away

in victorious defeat . . .
                thy last, resplendent spring.
Oh raise thy sunken head —
                now — in the triumph of extinction.

'Run for the Trovian shores' —
                for shores no longer seen . . .
And over the stiffening brine
                a solitary gull proclaims,

In a long and piercing cry —
                like the scream of an electric saw —
'thou, born from a wave,
                shalt become a wave of rock.'

THE END OF AN UNWRITTEN POEM

Song,
wild strawberry,
ripening dark —
the innermost
line
of the stream.

AN ELEGY ON THE DEATH
OF KENNETH PATCHEN

LAWRENCE FERLINGHETTI

A poet is born
A poet dies
And all that lies between
is us
and the world
And the world lies about it
making as if it had got his message
even though it was poetry
but most of the world wishing
it could just forget about him
and his awful strange prophecies
Along with all the other strange things
he said about the world
which were all too true
and which made them fear him
more than they loved him
though he spoke much of love
Along with all the alarms he sounded
which turned out to be false
if only for the moment
all of which made them fear his tongue
more than they loved him

though he spoke much of love
   and never lived by "silence exile & cunning"
      and was a loud conscientious objector to
         the deaths we daily give each other
           though we speak much of love
And when such a one dies
   even the agents of Death should take note
      and shake the shit from their wings
But they do not
           And the shit still flies
And the poet now is disconnected
          and won't call back
  though he spoke much of love
And still we hear him say
       "Do I not deal with angels
          when her lips I touch"
And still we hear him say
       "O my darling troubles heaven
         with her loveliness"
And still we love to hear him say
  "As we are so wonderfully done with each other
     We can walk into our separate sleep
       On floors of music where the milkwhite cloak
        of childhood lies"
And still we hear him saying
  "Therefore the constant powers do not lessen.
  Nor is the property of the spirit scattered
  on the cold hills of these events"
And still we hear him asking
  "Do the dead know what time it is?"

He is gone under
         He is scattered
              under sea
     and knows what time
         but won't be back to tell it
  He would be too proud
          to call back anyway
   And too full of strange laughter
         to speak to us anymore anyway

And the weight of human experience
        lies upon the world
    like the chains of the sea
                    in which he sings
And he swings in the tides of the sea
    And his ashes are washed
                in the ides of the sea
And "an astonished eye looks out of the air"
                        to see the poet singing there

And dusk falls down
                somewhere

        where a white horse
                        without a rider
            turns its head
                        to the sea

NOTES ON CONTRIBUTORS

WALTER ABISH'S work has appeared in, among other publications *New Directions 23, Extensions,* and *New American Review.* At present, he is finishing a novel based on "With Bill in the Desert."

The sculptor and concrete poet J-F. BORY edits the Paris magazine *Approches* and is the author of several "concrete" books, including the international anthology *Once Again* (New Directions).

The British poet EDWIN BROCK fashions his poems directly from his life's experience as a sailor, policeman, journalist, and adman, husband and father. His first collection, *An Attempt at Exorcism,* was published in 1959, and was followed over the next decade by *A Family Affair, With Love from Judas,* and *A Cold Day at the Zoo,* as well as a large selection in *Penguin Modern Poets 8.* This year, New Directions is bringing out *Invisibility Is the Art of Survival,* marking the first appearance in this country of Brock's poetry in book form.

One of Latin America's most widely read poets, ERNESTO CARDENAL was born in 1925 in Granada, Nicaragua. He entered the Cistercian monastery of Gethsemani, in Kentucky, in 1957, and until his departure two years later, was a novice under the late Thomas Merton. Subsequently ordained a priest, Cardenal returned to Nicaragua, where he now lives, directing a small monastic community at Archipiélago de Solentiname. His "Coplas" was occasioned by Merton's accidental death by electric shock in Bangkok, Thailand, on December 9, 1968. Merton's own renditions of Cardenal's poetry were included in *New Directions 17* and *Emblems of a Season of Fury* (NDP140); Herder & Herder, in 1971, brought out a collection entitled *Psalms of Struggle and Liberation.* MIREYA JAIMES-FREYNE, herself a poet, teaches at the University of California (Santa Barbara); KENNETH REXROTH is presently completing *Love Is an Art of Time,* a companion volume to his classic *100 Poems from the Japanese.*

Earlier this year, LAWRENCE FERLINGHETTI made a reading tour of Australia and New Zealand, accompanied by Allen Ginsberg and the Russian poets Yevgeni Yevtushenko and Andrei Voznesensky. His latest collection, *Open Eye*, is scheduled for publication in spring 1973, adding still one more title to the nine already on the New Directions list. "An Elegy on the Death of Kenneth Patchen" was first read on February 3, 1972, at the Kenneth Patchen Memorial Reading given by the City Lights Poets Theatre, and published two weeks later in *The Sunday Paper* (San Francisco).

BARENT GJELSNESS has been a teacher-lecturer in universities and community colleges for nine years, and is the editor of *Changes* (355 North Court Avenue, Tucson, Arizona 85702), an annual magazine of poetry, art, photography, interviews, articles, and short stories. Gjelsness himself has published poetry in such periodicals as *Intransit, Kayak, Lillabulero,* and *The Minnesota Review.*

PETER HANDKE was born in Griffen, Austria, in 1942. After graduating from a Catholic seminary in 1959, he studied law for four years at the University of Graz. Handke first attracted public notice with an unprecedented, yet soft-spoken, attack on contemporary German writing at the 1966 meeting, in Princeton, of the "Group 47." That year also saw the publication of his first novel, *Die Hornissen* ("The Hornets"), and his first stage success, *Publikumsbeschimpfung* ("Offending the Audience"). MICHAEL ROLOFF has translated all of Handke's work that has appeared in English so far: *Kaspar and Other Plays,* and the novel *The Goalie's Anxiety at the Penalty Kick* (Farrar, Straus & Giroux); the plays *My Foot My Tutor?* and *Calling for Help* (in *The Drama Review,* Volume 15, Number 1, Fall 1970); *The Ride Across Lake Constance* (in *Contemporary German Drama,* Michael Roloff, ed.; Avon Books).

E. W. JOHNSON, who now lives in Dunedin, Florida, edited the widely selling anthology *Contemporary American Thought* (The Free Press, 1968). Along with his dog, Samantha, he delights in charging furiously across the continent, engaging in bizarre adventure.

The Brazilian author OSMAN LINS was born in Pernambuco and now lives in São Paulo. He has distinguished himself in several fields of literary endeavor, and is a prize-winning playwright as well as an active essayist much preoccupied with the present state of Brazilian art and culture. *Studies in Short Fiction* (Winter 1971) featured an article by Anatole Rosenfeld, "The Creative Narrative Process of Osman Lins," pertaining to *Nove Novena* ("Nine Novena"), the collection from which "The Transparent Bird" is taken. CLOTILDE WILSON, the translator, is associate professor of French at the University of Washington in Seattle.

Born in Tchetchelnik in the Ukraine, CLARICE LISPECTOR emigrated to Brazil with her parents and spent her childhood in Recife, in the northeastern state of Pernambuco. After graduation from the National Faculty of Law in Rio, she began her career as a writer, publishing her first novel in 1944. Her steady output, including novels, short stories, chronicles, and stories for children, has won for her a number of important literary awards. Her novel *Apple in the Dark* (Alfred A. Knopf, 1967) is available in English.

Born in Berwyn, Illinois, TOBY OLSON lives in New York City and teaches at Long Island University and the New School for Social Research. His books include *Maps* and *Worms into Nails* (The Perishable Press) and *Pig/s Book* (Dr. Generosity Press). A new volume, *The Wrestlers and Other Poems*, is soon to be published by Barlenmir House, and he has recently finished a novel called *The Life of Jesus*.

JAMES PURDY's most recent novel, *I Am Elijah Thrush*, was brought out this past May by Doubleday, and appeared in an abridged version in the December 1971 *Esquire*. He is now working on *The House of the Solitary Maggot*, the second volume of his trilogy about Midwestern towns called *Sleepers in a Moon-Crowned Valley*; the first, *Jeremy's Version* (Doubleday), was published in 1970. New Directions has two Purdy collections on its list, *Children Is All* (stories and short plays) and *Color of Darkness* (stories).

MIA RAFFEL says about herself: "I live in Toronto . . . spent last year in Austin, Texas, writing a Mexican-based film script called *The Lizard* . . . now working on stories, more prose-poems, and a short lunatic film script on the Aztecs, to be called *Sacrifice* . . . recently my eyes turned from blue to green . . . in Canada I'm enjoying all the flying snow and trying to find out some things about the Indians and the Eskimos."

Last year, New Directions brought out CARL RAKOSI's *Ere-Voice*, his first collection of poetry since *Amulet* (1967). He was awarded a $5,000 fellowship, in 1972, from The National Endowment for the Arts. Rakosi—a leading member of the Objectivist Group that included, among others, Louis Zukofsky, Charles Reznikoff, and George Oppen—as ever seeks primarily in his work "to present objects in their most essential reality and to make of each poem an object . . . meaning by this, obviously, the opposite of a subject; the opposite, in other words, of all forms of personal vagueness; of loose bowels and streaming, sometimes screaming, consciousness."

Biographical information on ALEKSIS RANNIT will be found in the introduction preceding his "Dry Radiance." HENRY LYMAN—a poet, translator, and short story writer—lives in Bloomfield, Connecticut, and is presently preparing a volume of his English renderings of Rannit's poetry.

GARY SNYDER, a leader in the movement to save our natural environment, now lives in a house in the foothills of the Sierras in California that he built for his family two years ago. His most recent poetry collection, *Regarding Wave*, was published in 1970 by New Directions. A Bollingen Foundation grant recipient and Guggenheim Fellow, his other books include *Riprap* (1959), *Myths and Texts* (1960), *Riprap and Cold Mountain Poems* (1965), *Six Sections from Mountains and Rivers without End* (1965), *The Back Country* (1968), and *Earth House Hold* (1969).

ANDREA ZANZOTTO was born in 1921 in Pieve di Soligo (Treviso, Italy) and started teaching at the age of sixteen in a private school. In 1942, he was graduated in letters from the University of Padua. After World War II and completion of his military service, he traveled abroad to France and Switzerland, and upon his return to Italy resumed teaching in high schools of various towns of the Veneto region, although always residing in his birthplace. A man of rare culture and critical insight, he has written numerous critical essays, among them a notably brilliant interpretation of the work

of Henri Michaux. VITTORIA BRADSHAW, Italian born and now re-
siding in California, is an active translator, working in the English,
French, German, Italian, and Russian languages.

A TRIBUTE TO EZRA POUND

Since journals are edited in honor of James Joyce and William Butler Yeats among others, it is a pleasure to announce that a new journal has been formed in honor of Ezra Pound . . . too long neglected by too many professionals in 20th-century letters. *Paideuma, a journal devoted to Ezra Pound scholarship*, will appear as many times a year as high-quality material is available.

The editorial board includes such international Pound authorities as Hugh Kenner, University of California, Santa Barbara; Eva Hesse, Munich, West Germany; Donald Davie, Stanford University; Donald Gallup, Yale University; and Lewis Leary, University of North Carolina. Associates who will help in making the journal a real tribute to Ezra Pound include such people as William Cookson, London; Harry Meacham, Academy of American Poets, Virginia; and William Tierney, at Quebec, Canada. The editors and friends of *Paideuma* believe the time has come when Pound will begin to take his rightful place as the most important poet and man of letters of the 20th-century Western World. The managing editor, Carroll F. Terrell, can be reached for information at the University of Maine, Orono, Maine 04473.

New Directions Paperbooks

Eugenio Montale, *Selected Poems.†* NDP193.
Vladimir Nabokov, *Nikolai Gogol.* NDP78.
Pablo Neruda, *Captain's Verses.†* NDP345.
New Directions 17. (Anthology) NDP103.
New Directions 18. (Anthology) NDP163.
New Directions 19. (Anthology) NDP214.
New Directions 20. (Anthology) NDP248.
New Directions 21. (Anthology) NDP277.
New Directions 22. (Anthology) NDP291.
New Directions 23. (Anthology) NDP315.
New Directions 24. (Anthology) NDP332.
New Directions 25. (Anthology). NDP339.
Charles Olson, *Selected Writings.* NDP231.
George Oppen, *The Materials.* NDP122.
  Of Being Numerous. NDP245.
  This In Which. NDP201.
Wilfred Owen, *Collected Poems.* NDP210.
Nicanor Parra, *Emergency Poems.†* NDP333.
  Poems and Antipoems.† NDP242.
Boris Pasternak, *Safe Conduct.* NDP77.
Kenneth Patchen, *Aflame and Afun of
  Walking Faces.* NDP292.
  Because It Is. NDP83.
  But Even So. NDP265.
  Collected Poems. NDP284.
  Doubleheader. NDP211.
  Hallelujah Anyway. NDP219.
  In Quest of Candlelighters. NDP334.
  The Journal of Albion Moonlight. NDP99.
  Memoirs of a Shy Pornographer. NDP205.
  Selected Poems. NDP160.
  Sleepers Awake. NDP286.
  Wonderings. NDP320.
Octavio Paz, *Configurations.†* NDP303.
  Plays for a New Theater. (Anth.) NDP216.
Ezra Pound, *ABC of Reading.* NDP89.
  Classic Noh Theatre of Japan. NDP79.
  The Confucian Odes. NDP81.
  Confucius. NDP285.
  Confucius to Cummings. (Anth) NDP126.
  Guide to Kulchur. NDP257.
  Literary Essays. NDP250.
  Love Poems of Ancient Egypt. Gift Edition.
  NDP178.
  Pound/Joyce. NDP296.
  Selected Cantos. NDP304.
  Selected Letters 1907-1941. NDP317.
  Selected Poems. NDP66.
  The Spirit of Romance. NDP266.
  Translations.† (Enlarged Edition) NDP145.
Omar Pound, *Arabic and Persian Poems.*
  NDP305.
James Purdy, *Children Is All.* NDP327.
Raymond Queneau, *The Bark Tree.* NDP314.
Carl Rakosi, *Amulet.* NDP234.
  Ere-Voice. NDP321.
John Crowe Ransom, *Beating the Bushes.*
  NDP324.
Raja Rao, *Kanthapura.* NDP224.
Herbert Read, *The Green Child.* NDP208.
Pierre Reverdy, *Selected Poems.†* NDP346.
Kenneth Rexroth, *Assays.* NDP113.
  An Autobiographical Novel. NDP281.
  Bird in the Bush. NDP80.
  Collected Longer Poems. NDP309.
  Collected Shorter Poems. NDP243.
  Love and the Turning Year. NDP308.
  100 Poems from the Chinese. NDP192.
  100 Poems from the Japanese.† NDP147.
Charles Reznikoff, *By the Waters of Manhattan.*
  NDP121.

Testimony: The United States 1885-1890.
  NDP200.
Arthur Rimbaud, *Illuminations.†* NDP56.
  Season in Hell & Drunken Boat.† NDP97.
Saikaku Ihara, *The Life of an Amorous
  Woman.* NDP270.
St. John of the Cross, *The Poems of St. John of
  the Cross.†* NDP341.
Jean-Paul Sartre, *Baudelaire.* NDP233.
  Nausea. NDP82.
  The Wall (Intimacy). NDP272.
Delmore Schwartz, *Selected Poems.* NDP241.
Stevie Smith, *Selected Poems.* NDP159.
Gary Snyder, *The Back Country.* NDP249.
  Earth House Hold. NDP267.
  Regarding Wave. NDP306.
Enid Starkie, *Arthur Rimbaud.* NDP254.
Stendhal, *Lucien Leuwen.*
  Book I: *The Green Huntsman.* NDP107.
  Book II: *The Telegraph.* NDP108.
Jules Supervielle, *Selected Writings.†* NDP209.
Dylan Thomas, *Adventures in the Skin Trade.*
  NDP183.
  A Child's Christmas in Wales. Gift Edition.
  NDP181.
  Collected Poems 1934-1952. NDP316.
  The Doctor and the Devils. NDP297.
  Portrait of the Artist as a Young Dog.
  NDP51.
  Quite Early One Morning. NDP90.
  Under Milk Wood. NDP73.
Lionel Trilling, *E. M. Forster.* NDP189.
Martin Turnell, *Art of French Fiction.* NDP251.
  Baudelaire. NDP336.
Paul Valéry, *Selected Writings.†* NDP184.
Vernon Watkins, *Selected Poems.* NDP221.
Nathanael West, *Miss Lonelyhearts &
  Day of the Locust.* NDP125.
George F. Whicher, tr.,
  The Goliard Poets.† NDP206.
J. Willett, *Theatre of Bertolt Brecht.* NDP244.
Jonathan Williams, *An Ear in Bartram's Tree.*
  NDP335.
Tennessee Williams, *Hard Candy.* NDP225.
  Camino Real. NDP301.
  Dragon Country. NDP287.
  The Glass Menagerie. NDP218.
  In the Winter of Cities. NDP154.
  One Arm & Other Stories. NDP237.
  The Roman Spring of Mrs. Stone. NDP271.
  Small Craft Warnings. NDP348.
  27 Wagons Full of Cotton. NDP217.
William Carlos Williams,
  The William Carlos Williams Reader.
  NDP282.
  The Autobiography. NDP223.
  The Build-up. NDP259.
  The Farmers' Daughters. NDP106.
  Imaginations. NDP329.
  In the American Grain. NDP53.
  In the Money. NDP240.
  Many Loves. NDP191.
  Paterson. Complete. NDP152.
  Pictures from Brueghel. NDP118.
  The Selected Essays. NDP273.
  Selected Poems. NDP131.
  A Voyage to Pagany. NDP307.
  White Mule. NDP226.
Yvor Winters,
  Edwin Arlington Robinson. NDP326.
John D. Yohannan,
  Joseph and Potiphar's Wife. NDP262.

Complete descriptive catalog available free on request from
New Directions, 333 Sixth Avenue, New York 10014.   † Bilingual